ISLINGTON

Please return this item on or before the last date stamped below or you may be liable to overdue charges. To renew an item call the number below, or access the online catalogue at www.islington.gov.uk/libraries. You will need your library membership number and PIN number.

August 16

6.19

Islington Libraries

020 7527 6900   **www.islington.gov.uk/libraries**

D1343737

The Lost Sheenan's Bride

A Taming of the Sheenans Romance

JANE PORTER

TULE
PUBLISHING

DEDICATION

For my middle son
Ty Thomas Gaskins
I get you
and love you
more than you'll ever know

Dear Reader,

I confess, I put off writing *The Lost Sheenan's Bride* for a long, long time. It wasn't because I didn't like or know the story, but because I knew when it was finished, my *The Taming of the Sheenans* series would be complete, and it broke my heart a little bit. These tough Montana brothers have been with me for three years now. I started the first, Brock's *Christmas at Copper Mountain*, late summer 2013, and here we are, summer of 2016 saying goodbye.

I love connected stories, especially stories about families. My family is my world, and when I lost my dad at fifteen, it was my close relationship with my two brothers and sister that saw me through the loss and grief. Whenever I write about family, there is struggle and challenge, as well as change. Change is part of life. We can't avoid it. Which is why I create strong families that might not always see eye to eye, but when the chips are down, they show up to support each other through good times and bad.

Thankfully, endings also become beginnings, and with the closing of The *Taming of the Sheenans*, I introduce my new series, *The Douglas Ranch of Paradise Valley*. From reading *The Taming of the Sheenans*, you know the Sheenans and the Douglases lives are intertwined. They aren't just neighbors. McKenna Douglas and Trey Sheenan were high school sweethearts and have a complicated relationship (*The Kidnapped Christmas Bride*), and now with the *The Douglas*

Ranch of Paradise Valley, you'll get the rest of the story.

I'd love to hear from you. Please drop me a note any time to jane@janeporter.com, and do sign up for my newsletter so you can hear about all my future releases.

Happy summer! Happy reading!

Jane

Chapter One

THE GLASS DOOR swung open and then shut, sucking cold air and a flurry of snowflakes into Marietta's Java Café on Main Street.

Even before the heavy boots thudded on the wooden floorboards, Jet felt a rush of awareness, the skin at her nape tingling. *He was here.*

Jet Diekerhof sat up a little straighter, trying to act blasé, wanting desperately to be indifferent as she was so *over* men—finished, done with—but biology seemed to have a different idea because every time *he* was around, her brain lit up, synapses firing, body warming, skin tingling, screaming at her that the hottest guy she'd ever seen had just entered Marietta's coffee shop.

She didn't want to be interested. She didn't want to think about guys—hot, handsome men with hard bodies, sinewy biceps, and chiseled jaws—but it was impossible to ignore the crazy adrenaline rush when he was close by. And the adrenaline was surging now. Her hands shook and her skin flushed hot, before turning cold. Even her heart was beating double time.

Jet didn't know why he had this effect on her. She didn't know anything about him. Didn't even know his name. He was just gorgeous. Hot, sexy, smoldering, heart palpitation kind of gorgeous. He had a whole sleeve of tattoos—she thought that was what they called them when they covered an arm—and long, thick, dark hair and a dark scruff of a beard that made her stare at his mouth.

He had a sexy mouth. Sexy muscles.

But best of all—or maybe worst of all—he had a *brain*.

She never saw him without a stack of books, tons of books, and notebooks, and a laptop. He'd show up and turn his table at Java Café into a mini-office, books and notepad and laptop spread out around him, and he'd read, pen in hand, ready to jot down notes.

He was always scribbling something. She loved that. No, hated that. Hated that he fascinated her, especially when he'd sit there working with that fierce focus, oblivious to everything around him.

He had to be a teacher, a grad student, a writer. Something like that. Who else would sit for hours in a coffee shop, pouring over books, biceps beautifully bunched, brow furrowed in concentration?

He was intense and edgy and intriguing and she'd never met anyone else like him.

Not that she'd ever actually met him.

And not that she wanted to meet him. Men were trouble. Men were distracting and confusing and they'd break her heart and she wouldn't even see it coming.

So no. She didn't want to know him. She didn't even want to be aware of him, and yet her skin prickled with goose bumps, and her pulse was jumping...

But that didn't matter. She didn't care. She didn't care that he wasn't wearing a wedding ring, and that no one ever joined him at his table. She didn't care that he drank tea, not coffee, and that the café served him tea in a china cup. *With a saucer.*

And she most definitely hadn't fantasized about him. She hadn't pictured him dropping into a chair at her table, long muscular legs outstretched, big muscular torso angled carelessly away, even as his dark eyes watched her with sexy, lazy, delicious intent.

She didn't want that. She couldn't want it. Because the last time she'd been attracted to someone heart meltingly handsome he'd broken her heart and she wasn't going down that road again. She was only just starting to feel better. Just beginning to feel almost whole again but, even now, she could still feel the deep bruise in her chest where her heart should be.

She still didn't know if Ben had played her, or she'd been naïve, but either way, falling for anyone, much less falling hard, was dangerous and foolish.

But that didn't stop her from watching her mystery man cross the Java Café as he headed to the counter.

He was wearing old, faded jeans that hung from his lean

hips, jeans that outlined his hard quads and hamstrings before falling to the tips of his black boots. They weren't combat boots or cowboy boots, but something a guy who rode a motorcycle might wear. Bad ass. Take no prisoners.

And then he turned abruptly and his dark eyes—deep, deep brown, almost black—met hers and held.

Her heart fell all the way to her feet.

She went blistering hot and then icy cold.

She couldn't look away. She didn't know why. Maybe it was because he'd never once even glanced her way before, and now he was giving her a long, slow once-over and she didn't know what to do with that.

Hot again, cheeks burning, she finally dropped her gaze, grabbed the student papers in front of her, forcing her attention back to her grading. *Breathe,* she told herself, *breathe. Act normal.*

Not that she had the faintest idea what normal was.

Jet had never been normal.

Geeky, smart, happy, confident...she'd loved school from her first day of kindergarten. She'd excelled in every subject, all the way through elementary school, a perfect student on into junior high, winning prizes for most books read during the summer, ribbons in the annual essay contest and science fair. She'd been the quintessential book girl...even teacher's pet... and she'd thrived in school, all the way until the day in eighth grade when she overheard girls ridiculing her in the bathroom.

And they did it, knowing she was in there.

Knowing she was a captive audience in the stall.

They didn't stop, either, not even when she finally emerged; face blotchy from holding back tears.

She didn't cry while she washed her hands. She kept her chin up while she dried her hands. She walked out of the bathroom, head high.

It wasn't until she was home that she gave into tears.

She'd known since second grade she wasn't popular, but she hadn't realized how unpopular she was until that day. But Jet refused to change. If she was going to be mocked for being smart, she'd show them just how smart she was.

She studied harder than ever, never letting anyone know in high school that her amazing grades weren't effortless. She wanted the haters to think it all came easy, so she let them believe she whizzed through, and she did a pretty good impression of loving life, with her 4.4 GPA—thanks to all the AP and honors classes—and near perfect scores on the SAT and ACT.

But once she'd finished college—which had been a lot of work—she didn't know what to do with herself.

She didn't know what she wanted.

She'd spent so much of her life trying to prove she was smart and successful, that she didn't really even know who she was...other than smart, and academically successful.

After graduating, Jet earned a teaching credential, making sure to qualify as both an elementary teacher and a single subject teacher in English, social studies, science and math.

If she was going to be an overachiever, why not do it to the max?

But after a year of teaching she was more disillusioned than ever.

She wasn't sure she wanted to be in a classroom for the rest of her life. She felt as if she'd only ever been in a class-room—

"Can I join you?"

The deep voice was paired with denim clad legs and heavy, black boots.

Jet jerked her head up. Heart pounding, face hot, she looked into dark eyes.

Him. It was *him.*

"There are no open tables."

Her mouth opened, shut. "Sure." She choked, hands trembling ever so slightly as she gathered her papers and pulling her laptop closer, giving him space.

"You're fine," he said, setting his leather backpack on top of the empty chair. "Don't move your stuff."

"It's okay. I don't need—" She broke off, swallowing the words, since he'd walked away, returning to the counter to collect his order.

Blushing furiously, she forced her attention to the paper in front of her. She felt stupid and gauche and she wished she could disappear, and she kept her head down even as he placed the bagel and tea on the table and drew his chair back.

Focus, focus, focus.

"I'm Shane," he said, taking a seat.

Shane. Not *the* Shane…the one renting the Sheenan house…the one that had everyone talking?

"Jet," she replied, extending her hand, amazed at how calm she sounded because on the inside she wasn't calm.

On the inside she felt positively wild.

His hand closed around hers. One black eyebrow lifted. "Jet?"

His grip was firm, his skin warm, and she felt a little tingle all the way through her. "It's Dutch."

"You're the first Jet I've ever met."

"Then you need to go to Holland. It's a popular name."

"Are you Dutch?"

"Both sets of grandparents emigrated from Holland, some before WWII, and some after." Handshake over she slid her hand beneath her leg, trying to ignore all the crazy butterflies filling her middle, making her resent him for turning her into a gum-smacking teenager who couldn't handle herself.

"Did your parents speak Dutch at home?"

"To their parents, yes, but only a little bit with us kids. But our grandparents would only speak Dutch to us, which proved useful when I was traveling this year."

He nodded at the stack of papers in front of her. "You're a teacher."

She grimaced. "It's that obvious?"

"You're always grading papers." He paused. "Which grade?"

"All grades, K-8." So he'd noticed her before. Another shiver coursed through her. "I'm a long-term sub," she added, "at a one room schoolhouse in Paradise Valley. And you? What do you do? I always see you with a stack of books and papers."

"I'm a writer."

He had to be the Shane Swan renting the old Sheenan homestead then. She sat up a little taller, aware that the Sheenans were not happy he was in their home, but she didn't know why.

She'd like to know, though. "What kind of writing?"

"Nonfiction."

"That's a pretty broad subject area. You can squeeze a lot into that...biographies. History. Crime. War."

"Exactly."

"And so you write...?"

"History, crime, war."

Her eyebrows arched. "Pretty dark stuff."

"Can be. My job is to try to make it personal. Make people care."

"And do you?"

He laughed, flashing white teeth. "Sometimes."

"Have you been published?"

He hesitated. "I should have something out next year."

"That's great. Congratulations. I'll have to look for it. I

like nonfiction. That's kind of my thing to read."

"Oh, yeah? Any favorite authors?"

"Jon Krakauer… Sean Finley… too many to name them all."

For a moment there was a flicker in his eyes and then it was gone. His expression turned thoughtful. "Which Sean Finley?"

She frowned, thinking. "I've read virtually everything by Finley, but my favorite is probably the first one I read by him, the one on Custer's last stand. *Heartbreak & Heaven*."

"Why?"

"It was brutal. Sad. But really powerful. It's like reading about the Alamo. You know what's going to happen ahead of time, but the details in the retelling brought it to life and made the massacre that much more painful."

His mouth curved, and yet his dark eyes held hers, intent. "So you are Team Custer."

"No. More like Team Crazy Horse, but I feel for Custer. I do. He was foolishly brave and I had to respect him even though I didn't want to. The whole thing was tragic."

"He was in over his head."

"But I think most people are! I think most of us learn on the job…and we just kind of hope no one knows that we're wildly underprepared."

His smile widened. "Are you speaking from personal experience?"

Jet grimaced. "I might be in a little over my head at the

school, but I can promise you that no one will die on my watch."

"That's good."

A table was suddenly open across the café by the bay window. Jet watched Shane's face. He was going to head over there and grab the now empty table.

Her heart fell a little. It was absurd. She was absurd. There was no reason to like this man so much. She still knew virtually nothing about him. "I can watch your stuff if you want to claim it," she said.

He turned to look at her, amusement in his dark eyes. "I've worn out my welcome already?"

For a second she couldn't think or breathe, too lost in his dark eyes. He was really ridiculously good-looking. Too good-looking. She didn't like feeling so shallow.

"I just know you like your space," she said, and then blushed as one of his black brows lifted. "I mean, you never talk to anyone," she added quickly, "you just work."

He leaned forward, elbows on the table, biceps bunching beneath the smooth fabric of his gray Henley. "Is that why you never said hello?"

For a long moment she couldn't think of anything to say. "I've kind of sworn off men."

He looked at her, waiting.

She hurriedly added, "Not forever, obviously, but for awhile. Just until I have my confidence back."

"So it's not my tattoos. I thought maybe you weren't a

fan."

Jet's cheeks burned hotter. A dozen different emotions swamped her. But being the youngest in a big family had taught her some basic survival skills, and so she held his gaze, and kept her chin up. "I think you know you're…appealing."

He stared right back into her eyes for what felt like endless seconds before he lifted his cup, and took a sip, all without breaking eye contact. "I think you have plenty of confidence. You just need a little nudge."

Her breath caught in her throat. Her heart thumped. Tattoos and muscles and long, dark, wavy hair and ass-kicker boots…

Jet swallowed hard.

The black eyebrow lifted quizzically. He set the cup back down. "So what happened? Who stomped on your heart?"

Jet wished the floor would open up and swallow her whole. But it didn't. And Shane just watched her and waited for a response as if he had all day.

The silence stretched. Her heart thumped harder. Clearly he had all day.

"He's not important," she finally managed, struggling to sound careless and not at all sure she pulled it off.

"He must be if you've sworn off men."

"Maybe I am a little banged up." And then, dammit, her eyes filled with tears and she looked away and blinked hard and cursed him for making her cry.

She was so sick of being sad. So sick of being hurt. Ben McAllister wasn't worth it. He wasn't. She should be over him by now. But kind of hard to be over someone she loved deeply...

She swallowed hard and forced her attention to Shane. She looked him in the eyes. "Hearts get broken all the time. I'll be fine."

"Yes, you will." He smiled then, but the smile was kind.

Reaching into his leather satchel he pulled out a card. He placed it on the table between them before beginning to gather his things. "Should you ever want to get a cup of coffee, or talk books, or teaching—I used to be a high school history teacher—call me."

Jet watched him walk away, and take the still empty table by the bay window. He put down his tea and pulled out his laptop.

She turned to look at the business card he'd left on the table.

Sean S. Finley
Writer.

Stunned, Jet picked up the card. Sean S. Finley. *The* Sean Finley?

The card included a url for a website, a New York City PO Box, and a phone number.

She looked across Java Café to where Shane was spreading books around his laptop.

Couldn't be.

Could it?

She left her table, crossed the café to reach his table. "You're Sean?" she asked, flashing the business card at him.

"Sean is my pen name."

"You're him."

"Yes."

Her mouth opened, closed. "You could have told me."

"I did."

"Before I kept gushing."

He flashed a lazy white smile. "It was kind of nice to hear."

"I feel so stupid."

"Don't. Writers need feedback."

"Hmph." She crossed her arms over her chest and glared at him. At least she tried to glare at him but it was impossible when he smiled up at her like that. "Were you really once a teacher?"

"I was."

"Were you a good one?"

More white teeth. His dark eyes flashed. "I'd like to think so."

"Why did you stop teaching?"

"I sold my first book."

"*Heartbreak & Heaven*?" she asked.

He nodded.

"Was that really the first one you wrote, or just the first

one you published?"

"First one I wrote and published."

"Do you ever miss teaching?"

"Sometimes." His lips curved. "Like now. I always enjoyed the teacher staff room."

"Yeah, me, too." She knew she sounded mournful. "But when you're the only teacher in a one room schoolhouse, there isn't much of a staff room."

"Let's go to dinner Friday and you can tell me all about it."

Her pulse leaped. Her stomach somersaulted. The Sheenans would not be happy if they knew she was having dinner with him but, at the same time, this wasn't just any writer, this was Sean S. Finley. A literary rock star. A literary rock star that looked like a *real* rock star.

His dark eyes gleamed. His lips curved up in what could only be described as wicked. "We can swap teacher stories," he said.

Her heart was out of control. Doubt and misgiving warred with curiosity and fascination. "I'm still pretty new."

"And I've been out of the classroom for quite awhile. But we can talk books. And ideas. And what brought you to Marietta."

She shouldn't say yes.

She shouldn't.

And not just because Harley and the whole Sheenan clan would have a fit if they knew, but why risk making a fool out of herself? God knew she'd probably gush again, and talk about his books until he wanted to crawl under the table and die, but at the same time…she couldn't say no. He was one of her favorite writers. His books lined her keeper shelf back home in Visalia. How could she not want to talk to him more? Learn more about what he was working on now?

She smiled ruefully. "Okay."

"Where do I pick you up?"

"This isn't a date. Maybe I should meet you there."

"I was thinking we could go to Livingston. Have dinner at the Gallatin Steakhouse. Heard it's good. Have you eaten there?"

"No. But I've heard good things about it, too."

"I'll make a reservation, and there's no point driving separately. Unless, you're more comfortable, and if that's the case—"

"It's fine." She hesitated. "I'm not uncomfortable. I'll text you my number and my address and then you can let me know what time the reservation is for, and when you'll pick me up."

"Sounds like a plan."

HE SHOULDN'T BE doing this.

He shouldn't involve her.

Shane gave his head a slight shake as Jet walked away and he opened the Word document on his computer, the one labeled *DR 17*, his personal shorthand for Douglas Ranch,

Chapter 17.

But he didn't start working immediately. Instead he found himself staring blankly out the window, at a distant point across Main Street.

She wasn't what he'd expected.

He wasn't sure *what* he'd expected. It was obvious to all, she was pretty—cheerleader, homecoming queen pretty—with thick, gleaming, brown hair that hung past her shoulders, and light golden brown eyes with very black lashes. Her cheekbones were high and her lips were full and she had a flawless cream complexion. He'd anticipated that she'd sound much the same…a sweet, rather bubbly young woman without much to say.

But the moment Jet had opened her mouth she'd talked books and writing, and she proved to be well-read, too.

She had a mind of her own. Opinions. He liked that she was interested in history, as well as the world around her.

He liked her.

Which made him kind of hate himself for using her.

He was taking her out Friday to get information. Their dinner wasn't about her, but about her connection to the Sheenans, specifically Brock Sheenan.

Jet's sister, Harley, had married Brock Sheenan, the oldest of the five brothers, a couple years ago. The Sheenans were a wealthy, ranching family and had been ranching in Paradise Valley since the turn of the century, and Shane was living in the Sheenan homestead now, having leased it for a year. The lease would be up end of March, and at that time Shane would return to New York to finish his book. The book hadn't come together yet, there were pieces missing, but Shane was finding it difficult to focus on the Douglas ranch murders when there was another story surrounding him, one far more personal, one that had begun to haunt him night and day.

Shane exhaled slowly, aware that his pulse had quickened.

The Sheenans.

He could never think of them without a hard, tight knot forming in his gut. His chest was just as tight. Anger rolled through him, but then it was always there these days…simmering.

He hated them. Despised them. And yet after nine months living in their house, he was almost consumed with them.

They were far too compelling. But after all this time he shouldn't find them so compelling. Their mystery should be gone. The strangeness and novelty fading.

But the opposite had happened.

After spending nine months in Montana, he was more intrigued—and conflicted—than ever.

The family was universally admired. Well, maybe not Trey. He was the Sheenan who'd spent four years locked up after a fistfight killed a man. But the rest of the family, they were liked, and celebrated. Troy had given back the town the historic Graff Hotel, and Cormac had shifted his publishing and media companies from California to Marietta, filling a huge, old brick building on Main Street with the corporate offices.

Shane had learned a fair amount about the Sheenan brothers, and yet it was Brock, the eldest Sheenan, that remained the biggest puzzle. He was elusive, and distant, and yet he was the one that might be able to unlock the Sheenan secrets…that would possibly know what Shane wanted to know.

But Brock lived high in Paradise Valley and rarely came to town. If the Sheenan brothers wanted to see him, they went to him, on his ranch. Brock was the first to have moved out of the Sheenan homestead, and it was Brock who'd cut his father off as soon as he'd left home.

For eleven years there had been little communication between Brock and his father, and it wasn't until he'd married Harley that his new wife brought the two together again. By that time, Bill Sheenan was dying, and Harley managed to bring about a reconciliation between her husband and father-in-law, but from what Shane understood, it was probably too little, too late.

Shane wanted to know about the feud between Brock and Bill Sheenan.

Shane wanted to know about Brock's relationship with his late mother, Catherine Sheenan.

Shane wanted to know why Brock had become so antisocial and had removed himself almost permanently to his Copper Mountain ranch, high in the Absarokas.

The Sheenan family might be well-liked in the Marietta and Paradise Valley communities, but they weren't without their secrets and feuds.

Shane Swan was part of those secrets and feuds.

Only the Sheenans didn't know it yet. They didn't know anything about him, other than the fact that he was a writer working on a book about Montana history and he needed a place to work for nine months.

And all of that was true. He was a writer, and he had a nice deal for a book about the Douglas ranch invasion, a crime that had never been solved, but writing about the unsolved murders was really just an excuse to come to Crawford County and live in Paradise Valley, and observe the Sheenan family.

The family that was supposed to have been his family.

The family that chose instead to give him up.

Chapter Two

JET COULDN'T FOCUS. How could she after that conversation with Shane Swan, aka Sean S. Finley, *New York Times* bestselling author of six books? Books she'd read. And loved.

She did try, though.

She'd even shifted her chair, attempting to block him a bit from her view, but she could still see him in her peripheral vision at his table, his big muscular torso angled over his laptop, long lean fingers tapping away at the computer keyboard, thick black lashes shadowing his strong cheekbone.

Just looking at him made her feel a dozen different things—none of them emotions she wanted to feel. He was altogether too mysterious, too interesting, too complex, too exciting. Better to pack her things up and head back to Kara's house on Bramble Lane where Jet was renting a room. Jet's sister, Harley Sheenan, had found the place for Jet after she took the job teaching at the one room schoolhouse. Harley had also found the job for Jet. Harley was very much the classic first born, big sister, always taking charge, always doing the right thing. And in this case, the right thing was finding a job for her wayward, younger sister in the States.

Jet dragged her attention back to the one page essay in front of her, but almost immediately it wandered again.

So hard to concentrate with Shane at the window table.

But she had to concentrate. Semester ended last Friday and report cards were due to go home this week. She really wished the report cards had gone home before she'd started. It was awfully hard to judge progress based on the five and a half weeks she'd been in the classroom.

But she was grateful to Harley for reaching out about the teaching position in the first place. Jet had still been in Holland at the time, playing au pair for relatives in South Holland, outside Rotterdam. Jet hadn't gone to Europe to babysit, but to have a series of adventures, and she had. For four months. For four amazing months, she'd had an incredible time and then money ran out. Europe was so much more expensive than she'd anticipated and rather than return home, she'd gone to Holland where she played nanny for lots of second cousins in exchange for room and board. By Christmas, though, Jet was feeling restless and Harley's email about the teaching position outside Emigrant Gulch caught her attention.

Apply, Harley emailed. *Nothing ventured, nothing gained.*

When Jet didn't immediately respond, trying to image herself in Montana, teaching in a remote, historic, one room schoolhouse halfway between Marietta and Emigrant

Gulch—she'd had to Google the towns, they were so small—Harley shot off a second email. *What do you have to lose, Jet? It's only for six months and at least you'd be getting paid.*

That second email sealed the deal. Her savings was gone and her credit cards were full. She needed a paycheck.

Jet applied, was interviewed over the phone, and then interviewed again via Skype, and, after a background check, hired. Ten days later she was on a plane for Bozeman, arriving two days into the New Year.

After five and a half weeks in the classroom, she could honestly say she loved the job. While it was far more work than she'd anticipated—preparing five different subjects for six different grades was insanely time consuming—but she also had considerable freedom in terms of how to teach the subject matter, and she loved that. Jet loved kids and teaching. She found it really creative and fulfilling; and it was exhilarating not having administration hovering over her, judging her work, or criticizing her efforts.

There was talk that this was the last year for the Crawford County schoolhouse, as members of the community argued that taxpayers' dollars would be better served by putting the children on a bus and sending them to Marietta, but Jet hoped the school board would vote to keep the schoolhouse open—and not for her sake, but for the sake of history and tradition.

Across the café, a phone rang. Jet glanced at Shane,

watching as he answered. He leaned back in his chair, one muscular arm crossing his chest, the other holding the phone to his ear. Inky hair framed his strong brow and high cheekbones. His neatly trimmed black beard highlighted his jaw and beautiful mouth—

Sighing, she quickly stacked her books and papers and slid everything into her leather backpack and headed out of Java Café before she could look at Shane again.

She should have left a half hour ago.

Outside, Jet breathed in the cold, winter night, her breath clouding in the frigid air, and walked briskly to her car parked a couple blocks away, over by the mercantile. It was already dark even though it wasn't even five-thirty yet but she glanced up as she unlocked her car door, as if the jagged mountains, or snowcapped Copper Mountain, would be visible. If it was a clear night and the moon full, she would have seen Copper Mountain's peak rising behind the domed courthouse, but tonight's heavy clouds promised more snow. With or without snow, the turn of the century town was postcard pretty.

She could see why Harley had fallen in love with Marietta—well, okay, Brock Sheenan and his adorable twins—but also this community. Marietta, a little over a half hour from Bozeman, seemed to have everything, and although Harley had warned her about the cold and snow and ice, Jet loved it, preferring the dusting of white, to Central California with its months of gray from the tule fog, which could blanket the

San Joaquin valley from November through early March.

The only time Jet didn't love the cold was on the days the wind howled down through Paradise Valley, rattling the single pane windows in the one room schoolhouse. On those days the one hundred and seventeen year old, wooden building shook and shivered and everyone inside shook and shivered a bit. The kids rarely complained, though, hardened to Montana winters. Jet just pulled on her knit gloves and continued teaching, peeling her layers off as the day warmed.

It was a short drive from downtown to Kara's house on Bramble. Four blocks at the most, and it was a pleasant surprise to see Kara's car in the driveway. Kara, a Crawford County district attorney, worked long hours, and Jet really enjoyed Kara's company when she was around.

But entering the house, Jet heard voices coming from the living room. Kara wasn't alone. Quietly closing the door, Jet thought she recognized the voices. Sounded like one of the Sheenan brothers. "I want him out. I've wanted him gone since December."

"I don't think you have grounds to evict him," Kara replied. "But if you've gone to a month to month lease, just don't renew for the next month."

"So he'd stay another thirty days? Hell, no. I want Swan gone."

Swan. Were they talking about Shane?

Jet chewed her lip, suddenly uncertain if she should leave, or continue to her room. She didn't want to interrupt, but there was no way to get to her room without passing the others.

She opened the front door again and this time closed it hard, announcing her arrival, before walking briskly across the hall floor.

She paused in front of the living room, feigning surprise when she spotted Troy and Cormac Sheenan with Kara.

Conversation broke off and all three glanced her way.

"Hello." She smiled brightly. "Don't let me interrupt," she added. "I'm heading to my room to finish grading."

"We're just about finished," Troy said, rising. He crossed the room to give her a quick hug. "How are you? How was your day?"

He was tall, like all the Sheenans, and she had to tilt her head back to see his face. "School didn't burn down. Kids got home safely. I'm still standing." Jet glanced from Troy to Cormac. Cormac was on his feet, too, but he was frowning. He definitely wasn't happy. "How are two of my favorite Sheenans?"

"Good," Troy answered. "Just getting some advice."

"Kara is good for that," Jet agreed. "Talk on. I'll be at my desk, working, so I won't be in your way."

In her room, Jet dropped everything on the desk, and then peeled off her coat and kicked off her shoes before flinging herself on the bed, aware that Shane was the one renting the Sheenan house. He'd been on the Sheenan ranch in the foothills since last spring and, from the sound of it,

Troy and Cormac no longer wanted Shane there.

Were they evicting him? Or was something else happening? They'd clearly come to Kara for legal advice so whatever it was, it had to be serious.

Jet knew it was none of her business but she couldn't help worrying. The Sheenans had welcomed her into their family six weeks ago and they'd gone out of their way to include her in their Sunday dinners, special occasions, and family birthdays. If something had happened, she wanted to know, especially if there was something she could do to help.

But when Jet emerged from her room a half hour later to make dinner, Troy and Cormac were gone, and Kara was already in her bedroom, door closed, and didn't come out for the rest of the evening.

THE OLD SHEENAN homestead was quiet at night. But not empty.

Dillon Sheenan had warned him there was a spirit hanging around the place, and Shane had smiled grimly, wondering if the youngest Sheenan brother had been jesting, but after nine months at the ranch, living in the family ranch house, Shane had come to believe.

But Dillon had been wrong about one thing.

There wasn't one spirit here. There were several, although the dominant energy was feminine and nonthreatening. But even nonthreatening, Catherine Sheenan made herself known, determined to connect with him.

Usually Shane ignored her. He told himself he wasn't punishing her, but rather, he didn't know what to do with her. He told himself he wasn't angry with her, or his biological father, but that wasn't true. He was angry. He was deeply resentful as well.

Never mind hurt.

Maybe that was why his mother's ghost hovered around him.

Maybe that was why tonight she wouldn't leave him alone. He'd felt her from the moment he entered the kitchen to make dinner. She was weight and energy in the kitchen, filling the emptiness as if she were still alive and in human form.

"Go away, Catherine," he said, turning the heat off from under the cast iron skillet before plating his steak. "Not in the mood."

He carried his dinner—steak and a microwaved potato—to the family room, the only room with a TV, and dropped onto the old couch and turned the television on. He'd paid to have cable put into the house when he moved in last spring. He wasn't a big television guy but after two weeks of uneasy silence, two weeks of being watched by Catherine and friends, he decided cable was needed. And it had helped. It helped now.

Shane ate in front of the TV, flipping through channels, watching first David Muir cover the news, and then a recorded episode of *Last Week* with John Oliver, and then turned the TV off, giving up on entertainment for the night.

In the kitchen, he washed his dishes and the hair on his nape rose, followed by a ripple down his spine. She was here.

Watching.

Waiting.

But waiting for what? For him to acknowledge her? He'd done that.

Waiting for him to forgive her?

He didn't think he could do that.

Exasperated, he turned the water off, reached for a dish towel, and dried his hands. "Yes, Catherine?"

Silence greeted him. The silence felt unbearably sad.

His chest tightened. He swallowed hard. "Don't blame me," he muttered, tossing the now damp towel onto the counter. "You were the one that left me. Not the other way around."

But as he took the stairs to his bedroom, he could taste tears. Tears he never shed. He'd waited years for her to come back. She'd promised she'd come back and get him.

She never did.

JET WOKE UP to the smell of freshly brewed coffee and it got her out of bed immediately. Stepping into slippers, Jet pulled a sweatshirt over her flannel pajamas and headed to the kitchen where Kara was pouring herself a cup of coffee.

Jet nodded gratefully when Kara gestured to the pot.

"Would love some," she answered, smothering a yawn.

"You're up early," Kara said, handing Jet a steaming mug.

"Didn't sleep well," Jet admitted, wrapping her hands around the glazed mug, saving the warmth. "Weird dreams."

Kara pulled out a chair at the kitchen table and sat down. "What about?"

"The Sheenans."

"Why is that weird? Your sister is married to one."

"But this was different. This wasn't a dream where we're eating popcorn and watching a movie. The dream was intense. Stressful."

"How so?"

Jet splashed flavored creamer into her coffee and crossed the floor to sit down at the table across from Kara. "It's hard to explain, but in the dream they were in trouble, or there was trouble, and there was all this drama and worry. Even Harley was upset and she was running around, trying to fix things, or fix something, and I remember just feeling awful in the dream, and I woke up blue. And worried." Jet frowned. "I think it's because Troy and Cormac were here last night, and I know they were upset."

Kara wrinkled her nose. "Oh. Right. That makes sense."

"I know you can't talk about it, but Cormac was definitely not happy last night, and Troy was Troy…charming and friendly…but it was obvious something wasn't right."

Kara sipped her coffee, taking her time replying. "They'll

be fine. You don't need to worry."

"But there is something…wrong."

"You're right. I can't say anything. But if you're concerned, ask your sister. Or Brock. Maybe one of them will fill you in."

That wasn't going to happen, Jet thought, taking another sip. Harley was a great big sister but she was notoriously tight-lipped about all things personal, which was probably why she and Brock worked so well together. Neither of them were particularly touchy-feely, or into the baring of the souls. Jet doubted either of them would tell her anything, and she wasn't going to risk getting shot down. It was bad enough being the baby of the family without having the oldest family members put her firmly in her place.

Or what they perceived as being her place.

"Let me ask you something else," Jet said, hesitating a moment to pick her words with care. "Do you have a problem with Shane Swan?"

Kara's head lifted abruptly and she gave Jet a searching look. "I don't. No."

"You haven't heard anything sinister or bad. And knowing you, you'd be aware if he had a criminal past and you'd tell me if you thought he was a dangerous person."

Kara's stare became more pointed. "What's this about?"

"He's asked me to dinner Friday."

"Oh, Jet…"

"I said yes," she added quickly.

"I don't know if that's a good idea." Kara's brow creased. "Actually, I'm positive it's a bad idea. I think you need to tell Harley and Brock and get their input."

"They're not going to dinner."

Kara gave her a look.

Jet grinned. "I can imagine you cross examining people. It wouldn't be pretty."

"This is me being nice, Jet, and you and I both know that the Sheenans are not friendly with Shane Swan. They wouldn't be happy about you having dinner with him."

"Harley is married to the family, not me."

"You were just telling me last week how much you love those guys. That the Sheenans are so good-looking and smart and kind and that Troy is practically James Bond—"

"Stop. That's embarrassing. And I'm sure I only said it because I'd had a beer or two."

"You did say it."

"Then let's forget I said it, and this is just a talk about books and teaching and stuff like that. I'm sure he's not viewing it as a date—" She broke off as she saw Kara's arched brow. "He's not, Kara. Trust me."

"Where are you going for dinner?"

"Gallatin Steakhouse in Livingston."

"It's a date."

"It's not. Neither of us have ever been there and we thought it'd be fun."

"How are you getting there?"

She opened her mouth, then pressed her lips together without answering.

"He's picking you up," Kara said. "And I can tell you're determined to go, so don't say I didn't warn you when all hell breaks loose later."

"No one needs to find out."

Kara rolled her eyes. "This is a small town. Everyone will find out. *Trust me.*"

Chapter Three

J ET WAS WAITING in Kara's living room a few steps from the window when Shane pulled up in a burgundy Range Rover with lots of expensive, shiny chrome. The SUV looked new, and was nothing like the four-wheel drive trucks and SUVs most people drove in Marietta.

Shane's SUV shouted money, and Jet didn't know why his choice of car bothered her. All six of his books had been runaway bestsellers. One of his books had been turned into an HBO series and another one was in post-production for a big feature film. If he had money, and was successful, why couldn't he look it?

But she didn't like it, and the flashiness disappointed her. Her family was by no means poor. They were one of the largest dairy families in Central California and had weathered a lot of storms in the agricultural valley's challenging and changing economy, but her family's thrifty, practical values had apparently rubbed off on her whether she liked it or not.

Shane, dressed in dark jeans and a navy, wool coat open over a thin, gray sweater, was heading up the walkway even as she opened the front door. He looked effortlessly stylish and very New York. She couldn't help smiling. "You look very chic," she said.

"It's the buttons on the coat, isn't it?" he answered, holding one edge of the jacket out and inspecting it.

Her smile widened. "I think it's the hip length, and the stitching and buttons…all of it. But it's a good look."

He walked her to the Range Rover, opened the passenger door for her. "Sorry I'm late. Had car troubles. Just returned from picking up this loaner."

"So this isn't yours?" she asked.

"No. I'm more of a black truck no chrome kind of guy. Although I do have a weakness for cars made in the 1950s, my favorite being the 1957 Corvette. That's the next car I buy."

"What do you own now?"

"A 1958 Chevy truck. Matte black. Lowered." He flashed her a wry smile. "It does have a little chrome, but nothing like this rental."

She climbed into the Range Rover and he shut the door behind her before coming round the side to get behind the steering wheel. "What do you drive?" he asked.

She pointed to the silver-gray car parked just in front of the truck. "It's actually my sister's car. She's loaning it to me while I'm here. It's a Trax."

"A what?"

She laughed. "I know. I said the same thing when she

handed me the keys. It's a new compact SUV. Handles the roads great and gets even better mileage."

"If you have your sister's car, what is she driving?"

"Brock's big SUV, and he's driving his old truck again." Jet made a face as she smoothed her wine colored sweater dress over her thighs. She had tights on under, and knee high boots, but she suddenly felt a little naked. Shane was just so polished and sophisticated that she couldn't help feeling gauche, and so she kept talking, trying to cover her nerves. "I feel bad about that, but Harley says Brock never leaves the ranch, so it works out just fine."

"Why doesn't he leave the ranch?"

"He has his family there, and his ranch hands, and that's enough for him, I think."

"So you get a car. Pretty good deal for you."

"It is. I try to show my thanks by babysitting once a week for them—free of charge, of course—but I still feel guilty. Harley's my oldest sister and she's used to taking charge so at a certain point you just...give up...and go with the flow." She drew a quick breath, tried to slow her crazy pulse, as well as her chatter. "How about you? Do you come from a big family? Where are you in the birth order?"

He hesitated for a second. "Most of my childhood was spent in the foster care system."

She shot him a swift glance. "What happened to your parents?"

He laughed, a low, mocking sound. "Good question."

Jet couldn't look away from his darkly handsome profile, his firm lips twisted. She couldn't tell if it was a slash of anger or pain. "Are they still alive?" she asked hesitantly.

"No."

"That's why you went into foster care?"

"No. I was given to my grandmother, and when she died, I went into foster care."

Jet swallowed. "How old were you?"

"Four." He leaned forward and turned on the radio. "What do you like to listen to? Pop? Jazz? Alternative rock?"

He was shutting down the conversation. She glanced uneasily in his direction, wishing she hadn't probed as much as she had. "I noticed you didn't mention country." She was trying to be funny but it didn't come out quite as light as she intended.

He laughed that dry low laugh again. "You could be an investigative reporter, you know."

At least he didn't sound angry. "I've been told I'm far too curious for my own good. My brothers and sisters used to remind me all the time that curiosity killed the cat, too."

He shot her a swift glance, his jaw easing, dark eyes creasing at the corners. "And, no, I'm not really a country fan. But if that's what you want—"

"No. I like some of the new country, but I listen to everything, so I'm good with whatever you want."

He nodded, picked a classic rock station and drummed one hand on the steering wheel as he drove. Jet watched him from the corner of her eye, more fascinated than ever.

IT WAS GOOD he'd made a reservation. The dark wood-paneled restaurant was crowded, with nearly every table full, with clusters of adults waiting just inside the front door. Heavy, black iron chandeliers dotted the beamed ceiling, making the restaurant masculine and cozy at the same time.

Despite the line at the door, they were seated right away, and Jet couldn't help glancing at the tables they passed, noting the big steaks and plates of ribs and prime rib. Everything looked good and just the sizzling aroma made her mouth water.

"You're not a vegetarian, are you?" Shane asked, holding her chair out for her.

"No. But I've heard they have something for everyone here."

The waiter was at their table almost right away to take their drink order.

Shane looked at Jet. "Cocktail, wine, beer?"

"I'll probably have a glass of red."

"Me, too."

The waiter gestured to the wine list by the bottle. Again Shane looked to Jet. "I'm probably just having one glass," he said. "But I can certainly order a bottle—"

"I'm the same. I know they say it's a better value if you order by the bottle, but if you're not going to drink it, what's the point?"

As the waiter walked away, Shane leaned forward in his chair. "Are you thrifty?"

"I was raised to be."

"That doesn't answer my question."

"I might be a good investigative reporter, but you'd be a good prosecuting attorney."

His dark eyes shone. "And you still avoided the question."

She made a face. "I was supposed to spend a year traveling in Europe but after six months my money was gone and I had to come home. Not sure if that answers your question, *sir*."

"Are you always this feisty?"

"My parents would say yes."

"That pleases you."

Jet's lips curved. "I'm definitely not Harley. She is really solid...a really good person. Mature. Dependable. Salt of the earth."

"And you're not?"

"I'm not unreliable, but I'm not ready for a family. Not interested in settling down and having kids...at least not anytime soon. I want to explore the world. Have adventures."

"And Harley wanted to be a mom?"

"She was a mom. An amazing mom. Like the best. And then—" Jet broke off as her throat ached and her eyes burned, hot and gritty. She blinked hard and glanced away, staring across the dark restaurant until she was sure she could speak calmly. "She lost them in an accident. All three at once—" Jet reached up and swiped a tear before it fell. Her hand trembled as she wiped beneath the other eye.

"I'm sorry," he said quietly.

She nodded, blinking fresh tears. After a moment she added huskily, "It broke my heart. I can't imagine what it did to her."

"I can't imagine."

Jet exhaled. "It was the worst. The worst," she repeated. "That's how she ended up in Montana. She couldn't handle another Christmas at home without them, and so she took a temporary job on Copper Mountain Ranch and, well, the rest is history."

He studied her intently. "And she's happy now?"

"Brock and his kids love her. And they needed her. The twins had never had a mom. Their mom died when they were just babies, so Harley is really their mom now."

"You like Brock?"

Jet's brow creased as she suddenly remembered who she was talking to, and how Cormac and Troy were talking to Kara about Shane. There was definitely some bad blood between the Sheenans and Shane Swan and she was curious if it was one-sided, or if it was a mutual dislike.

"What do you think of the Sheenans?" she asked casually.

He shrugged. "I don't know them."

"You're living in their house, aren't you?"

For a split second his expression looked almost bleak, an odd light in his eyes, and then it was gone and Jet wondered if she'd imagined it.

"I rented the house from Dillon before he moved to Texas," he said flatly. "The others have kept their distance."

There was no change in his expression this time, but she felt a niggle from her sixth sense telling her something wasn't right and, for the first time since meeting him, she doubted him. There was more going on here. She wondered what would happen if she called him on it.

"I don't believe you." But she smiled as she said it, her tone deliberately light, having learned from being the baby in her family that it was essential to be strategic and as nonconfrontational as possible. The older ones would always help her if they didn't feel threatened.

Shane's black eyebrows lifted. "You're a very interesting young woman."

"What is going on with you and the Sheenans?"

"Maybe you can tell me."

"Is that a trick question?"

"No. I had no idea there was a problem."

Jet suddenly felt less sure of herself. "Come on."

"This is the first I've heard of an issue."

She felt another prick of guilt and unease. "Forget it," she said quickly. "Obviously I don't know what I'm talking about." She smiled tightly, relieved to see the waiter arrive with their wine. "What are you going to order?"

"Haven't even looked at the menu." He smiled faintly, his dark eyes boring into hers. "But I think you know that, too."

Too.

Jet reached for her wine and took a gulp, suddenly, dreadfully out of her element. She reached for the menu, opening it, trying to hide. Why had she even brought up the Sheenans? Not smart. If she was going to probe, she should have at least waited for dessert to save herself from an uncomfortable dinner.

"I liked Dillon," he said from the other side of the menu. "He seemed nice enough. I've never spoken to Brock. He's not in town much."

She lowered the menu an inch.

"I met Troy once, and he was okay," Shane added. "Haven't met Trey. And Cormac's an ass."

Her brow creased. "Cormac can be tough, but he's a great dad—" She broke off, gulped air, feeling the blood drain away. "And he's here," she whispered.

Not just here, but heading her way now.

Shane reached for his wine. "Is that a problem?"

Yes. "No." Panic bubbled up, making her heart pound and her head swim. She had to beat the panic down, telling herself she hadn't done anything wrong. She didn't know anything. No one had told her anything specific. There was no reason she couldn't have dinner with her favorite author.

And yet, as Cormac approached, she felt her legs turn to Jell-O.

It was all she could do to stand up and start towards him, determined to intercept Cormac before he reached their table. "Hey." She greeted him with a sunny smile. "Small world."

He hesitated a moment before kissing her cheek. "It is in this part of the country," he said, glancing past her, gaze locked on Shane. "Is that Swan you're with?"

"Swan?" She repeated, brow creasing.

He sighed. "Shane Swan."

"Oh, yes. We're having dinner. He's Sean Finley. Did you know that?"

"Yeah." But Cormac wouldn't return her smile. "And I'm not a fan, either. He's trouble, Jet. You shouldn't be out with him."

"Why?"

"I can't go into it now, but trust me. He's bad news."

"I'm not sure what he's done to earn his bad reputation, but he's been nothing but nice to me—"

"Did he ask you out?"

"Yes."

"Has he asked you about my family?"

Her mouth opened, closed. "Not sure what that means."

Cormac folded his arms across his chest. "He's using you. He's trying to get close to the Sheenans—"

"Don't you think that's a bit presumptuous?" she interrupted. "Can an attractive man not be interested in me, for me?"

"Yes, but that's not what's going on with Swan. He has an agenda—"

"And you don't, Cormac?"

"No. I don't." He frowned down at her. "Why would you say that? We've never had any problem..." His voice faded and he again looked past her, expression darkening. "What did Swan tell you?"

"About what?" She was so frustrated she wanted to stamp her foot, and she wasn't the type to stamp a foot. She couldn't do that in her family. The Diekerhofs had a zero tolerance policy for drama and tantrums. "I have no idea what's going on. No one has told me anything. There's just lots of hush-hush-hush but nothing that I can make sense of, and I'm not going to be rude to someone who has been nothing but nice to me without a really good reason."

Cormac took her arm and drew her from the center of the restaurant to a corridor on the side. "And he really hasn't asked you about the Sheenans?"

He asked the question looking hard into her eyes and she gulped a breath, heart falling. There was no way she could lie to him. That would only alienate him completely. "We did talk about Harley, but that's because I brought her up."

"And he said nothing about Brock? Or any of my brothers?"

Her unease grew. "Brock came up, too, when he said

he'd never met Brock. Or Trey. Just you, Troy, and Dillon."

"Did he mention McKenna?"

"No. Why?"

"Because he's writing a book about McKenna's family."

Jet gave her head a slight shake. "But why?"

Cormac seemed perplexed by her question. "You know about McKenna's family?"

"No."

He hesitated so long that Jet knew it was bad, whatever it was.

"There was a home invasion on the Douglas ranch when she was a little girl," he said gruffly. "Five members of her family were killed, including her parents, and a baby sister. The crime was never solved."

"Actually, I did hear about a mass murder on a ranch in Paradise Valley a long time ago—one of my students mentioned it—but I didn't realize that it was McKenna's family." She hesitated, perplexed. "And you're sure Shane's writing about it?"

"Yes."

"How do you know?"

"Back before Christmas I was in the house and saw the dining room at the house—my family home, the place I grew up in—and he'd turned it into his study. The walls were lined with bulletin boards covered with newspaper headlines."

She looked away and chewed on her lower lip. She didn't

know what to say anymore.

"He's interviewing people, too. Asking questions. It's not good. It's just stirring up a lot of bad memories." Cormac gave his head a faint shake. "Let me take you home. You don't want to be part of this."

She hesitated, trying to understand. "Part of what?"

"This…circus."

She still didn't understand. "He's a very respected writer. He's won a National Book Award—"

"It doesn't matter. He shouldn't be writing that book, in our home. So let me take you back to Kara's. I don't think it's good for you to be associating with him."

"Cormac, he's a writer, not a criminal."

"He deceived us. He said he was writing a book about Paradise Valley history…never about the Douglases."

"Okay, he has questionable judgment, but I don't think he's a bad person."

"Do you know what a book like this will do to McKenna?"

"But what if Shane can solve the crime?"

Cormac's jaw just tightened.

She reached out to give his forearm a squeeze. "What if he finds out something that could help the case? It's possible."

"And he'll make a fortune off it, too," he added bitterly.

"Make a fortune from what?" a deep, sardonic voice asked, interrupting the conversation.

Jet spun around, flushing hotly as she spotted Shane standing right behind her. How much had he heard?

She forced a quick smile. "Hey. We were just talking about you."

Shane smiled back, but the curve of his lips was faint and his dark gaze wary. "So I gathered."

Jet gestured to Cormac. "You know each other?"

The corner of Shane's mouth lifted a fraction, and yet it only seemed to make his expression harder. "We've spoken. Briefly."

Cormac eyed Shane coldly. "Still waiting on that departure date, Swan."

Shane shrugged. "Don't have one."

"The lease is not being renewed."

"The lease stipulates I'm to be given a thirty day notice, Sheenan. *Written*. Haven't gotten that."

"I would think it's uncomfortable remaining someplace you're not wanted."

"*You* might think so, yes. But I've spent most of my life in homes where I wasn't wanted, so..." His voice trailed away. He shrugged carelessly, holding Cormac's gaze the entire time.

Although Cormac and Shane were approximately the same height with an athletic build, Cormac carried more muscle, but if push came to shove, Jet sensed Shane would have no problem holding his own. And right now it felt very much like push would come to shove. The tension was so thick that Jet had to drag the air into her lungs. This was not good. If she didn't act quickly things were going to get out of hand.

She grabbed a hold of Shane's sleeve, and gave it a tug. "Come on," she said briskly. "We haven't ordered and I'm starving."

But Shane didn't seem to hear her. He was too intent on staring Cormac down. And Cormac was welcoming the challenge.

Bad.

Cormac wasn't one to trifle with. He might be the only fair Sheenan, but he and Trey were the family fighters. And glancing at Cormac, she could believe it. His jaw had thickened. His blue gaze glowed fire. The man's testosterone was flying.

"That's fine," she added, trying a different tactic. "If you're no longer interested in dinner, Cormac can just take me home. He offered—"

"I asked you to dinner. I want to have dinner with you," Shane retorted, cutting her short.

"Then have dinner with me, but this isn't dinner. So, either let's go sit down or I'm leaving." Her lips compressed. She was serious, too. She wasn't about to be pushed around by either of them.

Shane's dark head inclined, and he took her hand in his, fingers interlacing. "Let's eat." And without a backwards glance, he led her away from Cormac and back to their table.

SHANE COULD FEEL Jet's pulse as he walked her back to the table. It was fast. She was upset. He felt a pang of remorse. He needed Jet's help, but this wasn't the way to get her on his side.

He held her chair for her and then scooted the chair forward as she sat down. She murmured thanks but he could see from her pallor and the set of her full lips that she was far from happy. He wished he could blame Cormac, but her frosty tone back there in the restaurant corridor had been directed at him.

"I'm sorry," he said gruffly, taking his seat again.

"That was really uncomfortable," she said, staring at him, head high, shoulders squared, her wide, blue eyes unblinking, expression full of censure.

School teacher censure.

He would have smiled at any other time, but right now wasn't the time. He'd hurt her feelings and he didn't like it. He wasn't sure how to make amends, but he wanted to. Not because he needed her support but because he liked her. She wasn't just a pretty young thing, but a really nice person. A good person. And she deserved to be treated well.

And he really didn't want to smile, but she kept glaring at him, giving him the most reproving look, as if she weren't just a teacher, but a Sunday school teacher, and Shane couldn't remember the last time anyone had stared him down, letting him know in no uncertain terms that he was *in trouble*. And this was *serious*.

God only knew he'd experienced his share of angry teachers. Even as a boy, he'd known what not to do, but that was too easy. Why do what he was supposed to do? Why not do what he wanted to do? Why not do the thing that interested him?

He struggled to think of a suitable topic, hoping a change of subject would smooth things over. "How is the wine? Good?"

She wasn't done scolding him. "You were not helping things back there."

He'd apologize to her, but not for the interaction with Cormac Sheenan. Cormac had been making waves for Shane ever since Cormac arrived in town last November with his daughter, Daisy. He'd even gone so far as to contact Shane's agent and publisher. "Sheenan was attacking me."

She just looked at him, not the least bit sympathetic. "So?"

"I wasn't going to just stand there—"

"Why not? You're a man, not a child. I'm sure you've dealt with criticism before."

Shane no longer felt like laughing. "Ouch."

She shrugged impatiently. "I'd say the same thing to him, if he were here."

"But he's not."

"That's right. So I'm talking to you." She studied him a long moment. "Is it true? What he said? That your new book is about McKenna's family?"

"It's about the crime that was committed on the Douglas ranch, yes."

For a split second she looked surprised...no, disappointed, and then her expression went blank.

He wished he hadn't seen the disappointment.

He wanted her to smile at him again, which surprised him because he usually didn't give a rat's ass about what anyone thought, much less thought of him.

He shifted uncomfortably, arms folding over his chest. "I didn't like seeing him pull you out of the dining room," he said after a moment. "It looked rough, and so I went to check on you. Make sure you were alright."

There was a flicker in her blue eyes but her guard remained up. "I can usually handle myself alright."

"So I'm discovering."

She cracked a smile. "I've a mean left hook."

"Who taught you that?"

"My brothers. Just in case." Her smile widened. "It's proven useful more than once."

"I can imagine." Shane smiled at her. "And I am sorry for what happened back there. I shouldn't have put you in the middle."

She nodded, but her smile slipped. "I'd read your book coming out next year already has a movie deal." She toyed with the stem of her wineglass a moment before adding, "And that book is the one about the Douglas...crime...?"

Worry shadowed her eyes. The strange tightness in his

chest was back. He didn't know what she was doing to him, but he couldn't remember when he last felt so ambivalent about anything. "Yes."

"What kind of movie?"

"I'm not sure."

Her eyebrows arched.

"It depends on the producers. Could be a network series, or a major motion film. They're waiting for the book."

"But it's been optioned. For over six figures."

He nodded.

She looked away, her fine, dark brown eyebrows tugging, teeth sinking into the bottom lip. She was struggling. She strongly disapproved but she didn't know what to do about it.

Not yet, anyway.

"Jet, can I ask you something now?"

She looked at him, nodded briefly.

"If you didn't know McKenna, or the Sheenan family, would you think the book is such a terrible thing?" he asked.

She thought about it for a moment. "It depends on how it was written. If it's graphic and written for shock value—" She broke off, staring at him, seemingly more perplexed than ever. "Is it graphic?"

"There's no way to write about the massacre of a good ranch family without an element of sensationalism. It's a horrific, violent story. A tragedy." He hesitated. "That's never been solved."

"Why hasn't it been solved?"

He studied her a moment. "My opinion, or what the 'experts' say?"

"I would assume after a year or more of research you've become an expert."

He liked her more and more. "The investigation was poorly organized, with incompetent detectives. Huge mistakes were made right away. Critical ones that doomed the investigation from the start."

"Intentionally?"

"No. Paradise Valley is just rural and remote. No one had ever encountered anything of this magnitude. None of those who responded were adequately prepared for what they found, the result being a compromised crime scene." He drank from his wine goblet then returned the glass to the table. "It's a tragedy on top of tragedy, and it's bothered me ever since I first heard about it."

"So you decided to write about it."

"I decided to see what I could find out."

"Do you think you know who…did it?"

He hesitated. "I've begun to piece together my conclusion."

Her eyes widened. "Seriously?"

"Mmm."

"But I have to read the book, right?"

He chose not to focus on the sarcasm, teasing her instead. "You said you liked my books."

"I do. But this one is different. It's essentially a true crime story."

"Most of my books have been. Some just are man against man, while others are man against nature, but they are all crimes if you think about it. Tragedies, every one."

"What drew you to *this* story?"

"The same thing that draws me to every story. What really happened? Who were they? And what is true? My job is to piece together not just the story, but the truth."

She was studying him intently, looking at him as if she could somehow see into him, almost as if looking for his story, his truth. "Have you ever given up on a story?"

What an interesting question. He'd been interviewed many times in his career but he couldn't remember if he'd ever been asked that question.

"No." He reached for his menu, and flashed her a reckless smile, a smile he'd mastered as a fourteen-year-old when hauled before a judge to receive a punishment for running away from his 'home,' which was nothing more than an institutional care facility for boys with nowhere else to go. "Because that would be like giving up. And I'll never do that."

Chapter Four

J ET WAS FASCINATED with Shane.

She'd never met anyone like him before, and doubted she'd ever meet anyone like him again. He was an original. And she just wanted to know more. But he wasn't an open book, deflecting attention from his personal life to safe topics like novels and movies and the places they'd both traveled. She liked all those subjects so it was easy to talk about what she'd been reading and the spots she'd visited during her recent European adventure, but after a half hour of pleasant conversation, she was tired of discussing the best hostels in Ireland and wanted to learn more about him…whether it was Shane or Sean.

"How did you come up with your pen name?" she asked, as their dinner plates were cleared.

He waited for the server to leave. "It's actually an old family name."

"Which part?"

"All of it."

"Does the S in Sean S. Finley stand for Swan then?"

"Possibly. But maybe not." He saw her expression and

added, "The name was changed on my birth certificate, so I have my original name given to me at birth, and then the name on the amended birth certificate."

"Who changed your name?"

"According to Montana records, my parents. Their names and signatures are on the petition."

"What did they change?"

"My last name."

"Why?"

His lips curved but there was no warmth in his eyes. "That is the million dollar question."

"You have no idea?"

"I have an idea, but no supporting evidence."

"So your pen name, is it the name you had on the original certificate?"

"Not exactly. But it's a variation. My grandmother did not read or write well. She could do basic math but reading and writing were quite difficult for her, and so when she'd take me to the doctor, she'd give them my name but would never check or correct the spelling. So if you looked at my various medical records you'd see that my name is different on each—Sean. Shane. Swan. Finley."

"What did your grandmother call you?"

"Shane. Sean. Swan. Finley." He smiled faintly. "I think I was all of those. But usually Shane Swan or Sean Swan."

"Who was Swan?"

"That was my grandmother's maiden name. She was a

member of the Salish and Kootenai Tribe. The reservation is near Flathead Lake."

"I'm not familiar with the tribe."

"Not many people outside Montana and the Pacific Northwest are."

"Did she live on the reservation?"

"Yes."

"But you weren't born on the reservation?"

"No. I was born in Marietta, at their hospital over by the rodeo and fairgrounds." His smile turned grim and he turned his spoon over. "But I never went home with my birth parents. There was a complication at birth so my mother and I were both kept at the hospital for a week, and then my mother went home while I remained for another week, and then her mother came for me—supposedly because my mother was too weak to care for me."

Jet waited for more but he said nothing else. "You've clearly learned the art of cliff-hangers."

He laughed once, deep and low. "My grandmother took me with her back to Flathead Lake. She raised me until I was four years old."

Jet tried to hide her shock. "And you never saw your parents again?"

"Apparently my mother used to come see me once or twice a year. She had a small cabin at Cherry Lake—" He broke off. "Are you familiar with Cherry Lake?"

She shook her head.

"It's a little town on Flathead Lake, just south of Big Fork, before you come to Polson. Apparently my mother would come to the cabin with the other children and sneak away to see me."

"Do you remember her?"

"Barely."

"What do you remember?"

"I'm not sure if I remember her, or the pictures I've seen of her. She was very striking. Long, dark hair, high cheekbones, hazel eyes with these incredible black eyelashes that were so dark and thick, I think they had to be fake." He paused. "She was supposed to come back for me. That's the part I remember clearly. I refused to be adopted, would never even consider it, because she was going to come for me."

He didn't say anything else. He didn't have to. Jet knew the rest. His mother didn't return, and he grew up without a home, his childhood spent waiting for this fantasy mother to claim him. "I'm sorry."

His mouth tightened. Creases fanned from his eyes. "Me, too."

"And your father?" she asked, not certain she should probe but wanting to know the answer.

"Who knows? He is part of that million dollar question."

"He wasn't Native American?"

"No."

"Where is he now?"

"Dead. Both my parents are gone."

"You said your mother would bring the other children with her to Cherry Lake. That means you have brothers and sisters."

He was silent so long she didn't think he was going to answer, and then he looked up, right into her eyes, his expression shadowed. "Brothers, yes."

She suddenly saw a glimpse of the boy he must have once been—quiet, dark-eyed, introspective, and probably quite sensitive. "Have you tried to find them? Do they know about you?"

"Yes, and no. It's complicated. But life is full of mysteries. Sometimes we get lucky and find the answers, and sometimes we don't. Maybe that's why I write."

"It makes sense." Jet paused to take the menu from the waiter but she didn't even glance at the options, too interested in Shane. "How old were you when you knew you were a good writer?"

He was looking down, his gaze skimming the menu. "I don't remember," he answered, sounding almost careless.

She didn't believe him, not for a minute. "Really? No idea at all?"

His dark head lifted and he gave her a piercing look. "You sound like a teacher again."

"Good. I am one."

This earned her a reluctant smile. "Apparently, I learned to read early and seemed to always be writing. I wrote my first story the year after I went into foster care."

"Do you remember the story?"

"*The Raven and the Swan.*"

His tone was sharp and mocking, as if he was somewhat embarrassed of the boy he'd been. She hated that, as he must have been absolutely lovely…lonely, but lovely. "What was it about?"

His dark eyes met hers and held. "You're very persistent. Are you always this curious about everyone?"

"If it's someone I'm interested in. And I am interested in you. Not because you're Sean S. Finley, but because you're Sean Shane Swan Finley." She smiled at him to hide the fact that her chest felt tender and a funny little lump was growing in her throat. He had not had an easy life and yet he'd achieved so much. It really was remarkable. *He* was remarkable. "So tell me about your story, *The Raven and the Swan.* What do you remember about it?"

"It was a story of a little bird taken from his nest and told he could no longer be a raven anymore."

Oh. Jet swallowed hard. The lump in her throat grew.

"It was a very simple little story," he added lightly, the mockery back. He had no patience for the child he'd been. "Not much to it. The raven just wanted to go home."

His impatience with who he'd been bothered her, almost as much as the aching innocence of his story.

She blinked, eyes hot and gritty. "You're going to make me cry."

"Don't. The raven eventually became a swan. It all

worked out fine in the end."

She reached across the table and touched his arm. His skin was so warm she felt a crackle of energy race through her. "You don't like being a swan?"

His gaze was on her hand where it rested on his wrist and she drew her hand back, fingers balling, still able to feel the sizzle of heat.

"I am who I am," he said. "I can't dislike being Shane Swan, just as I can't dislike the childhood spent as a raven. They are all me…good and bad."

"I admire you."

"Not sure I deserve that."

"I am." She studied him a moment, seeing past the long, black hair, the dark beard, the hard handsome features, and realizing he was very much a self-made man. "I don't know if you get asked this all the time, but would you be willing to come talk to my students before you leave Marietta? I think it'd be so inspiring for them to hear you talk."

"And what would I say?"

Her shoulders shifted. "Whatever you wanted to say. You could talk about your past, your books, your life as a writer…the fact that you were born right here in Marietta at the hospital, just like most of them were."

He glanced from her hand up into her eyes. "I don't know that that would be such a good idea, the Marietta part. It's probably better to leave my convoluted past in the past."

"But you'd consider coming in to the school?"

"If you don't think I'd bore the kids too much."

"Impossible. There's nothing boring about you. They'll love you." She smiled. "They'll be fascinated by you and will probably have a ton of questions for you. But to be honest, they might ask you more about your tattoos than your writing."

"I'm happy to come in. I'd love to see you at work. I have a feeling you're a great teacher."

"Average—"

"Not average. Not in any way."

Her heart skipped a beat and her stomach did a little somersault. She could still feel the tingle in her fingers where she'd touched him. Her body seemed to light up around him.

Not true.

It wasn't just her body. She lit up around him. There was something about him that made her feel very aware...very alive. "Teaching wasn't my first choice," she said, drawing a deep breath, trying to slow her rapidly beating pulse, trying to stay levelheaded. Even though she'd tried to keep her guard up, he was getting to her...getting under her skin, and making her feel. Making her care. Not for the author but the man. Shane Swan. Raven.

"I wanted to study film," she said briskly, thinking a change of subject would be good about now. "It was my passion in school. But my parents wouldn't hear of it. They'd send me to college, but I needed to study something worthwhile, not something frivolous."

"Film isn't frivolous."

"It's not going to save the world."

"And you're supposed to save the world?"

"Well, I'm supposed to do my part."

A black eyebrow lifted. "What about your sisters and brothers? Are they missionaries or something?"

Jet grinned. "No. My brothers are dairy farmers. One of my sisters married a dairyman. And, well, you know Harley."

"What did Harley study in school?"

"Ag-business. And then she married a dairyman, too."

He grimaced. "So you're supposed to teach until you marry a dairy farmer and have babies of your own?"

Her nose wrinkled. He'd pretty much nailed it, but she didn't want him to thinking badly of her parents. They were good people, kind, hard-working, self-sacrificing. They'd passed on their values, and taught her the importance of tenacity and self-reliance. "It's not a bad life."

"No. *If* that's the life you want." He paused. "Is it?"

She glanced away, looking out across the restaurant, which was beginning to thin out. Many of the tables were empty. Waitstaff was clearing dishes off other tables. It must be getting late. "No."

"What do you want?"

Her shoulders lifted and fell. It was her million-dollar question. Once upon a time she had an answer—she wanted to marry Ben and have a family and be happy. And then she thought she was pregnant—obviously not a good thing—but Ben's reaction had shocked her. Instead of calmly discussing options, he'd given her an ultimatum—she could pick him, or the baby, but not both.

She was devastated.

He loved her enough to make love to her, but not enough to stand by her when *his* birth control failed.

When her period came ten days later, she was relieved, but still crushed. Ben was not the man she'd thought he was.

Ben, for his part, didn't see the problem. He hadn't wanted a baby, and Jet wasn't pregnant, so why all the drama?

I told you from the very beginning I didn't believe in abortion, not for me. She'd told him, fighting tears, still so hurt and disappointed and angry. Yes, angry. He'd lied to her. He'd agreed with her, he'd told her he'd never ask that of her...

Jet drew a slow breath now, and looked up into Shane's dark, watchful eyes. "I don't know what I want anymore. I just know what I don't want."

"And what is that?"

"Liars. Cheaters. Scoundrels." Her lips curved and she ground her back molars to keep the tears at bay. "And dead-end jobs without creativity or adventure."

His expression turned thoughtful. "And now you're here in Montana."

"I'm here in Montana," she agreed. "And I like my job.

I'm glad I'm here. No matter what happens in June, at least I had this adventure."

"What happens in June?"

"The teacher on maternity leave could return. The school board might decide to close the school. Or… I might be offered an extension of the contract."

"Would you want an extension? Do you like teaching at a one room schoolhouse that much?"

"I don't have anything else lined up, and it is interesting. And challenging." She grinned and the shadows in her eyes disappeared. "And when I'm not stressed out of my mind…fun."

IT WAS THAT moment her expression lit up, light dancing in her eyes that Shane realized he just might be in trouble.

He hadn't wanted to like her, but she was impossible to dislike.

She was, to be precise, rather irresistible.

Manhattan was filled with sleek, smart, gorgeous young things, but Jet had something he rarely encountered.

Sincerity, coupled with magic. It was a rather dazzling combination, and it lit her up, made her shine, making him think of fairy lights strung in the limbs of a gnarled oak tree. She had roots and strength and yet she also had light…a pure, shimmery light, and right now, sitting across from him, she sparkled and glowed in the night.

If she wasn't Harley Sheenan's sister, he would have

leaned across the table and kissed her.

He wanted to kiss her. He wanted to feel her mouth and breathe her in and taste her. Her lips were full and soft...the darkest pink...and he wondered how her lips would feel against his.

He didn't want to use her, either. Didn't want to.

He wished he could protect her. From himself. As well as the rest of the dangers in the world.

She didn't know he was a danger. He hoped she didn't trust him. He hoped her small-town upbringing had prepared her for wolves in sheep's clothing.

"Who was the liar and cheat?" he asked.

The light in her eyes immediately dimmed. Her lips compressed, her expression shuttered. "And the scoundrel?" Her tone was mocking. "My boyfriend. Of two years."

He hadn't planned on asking the question. It just popped out. But maybe it was the right thing to say. She was leaning back now, her shoulders rigid, her guard back up.

"So he cheated on you?" he asked.

"Worse than that." She looked past him, gaze fixed on a distant point across the restaurant. "He knew what I believed. He knew how I felt about something. We'd both agreed." Her head turned and she looked Shane in the eye. "But it was a lie. He didn't mean it. He had no integrity. None whatsoever."

"Had he promised to marry you?"

She laughed out loud. Shaking her head, she tucked a

long tendril of glossy brown hair behind her ear with the delicately beaded hoop earring. "*No.*" Still smiling she reached for her water glass, took a quick sip. "We'd been together, as I said, two years, and I thought I was pregnant. I told him. And before I could even go to the doctors and get it confirmed, he gave me an ultimatum. It was him, or the baby, not both. I had to pick."

Her lips curved up, high, even as fire blazed in her blue eyes. "And that would be fine, if he hadn't agreed before we ever slept together that abortion was *not* an option, at least, not for me. He knew how I felt, and he said those were his same beliefs." She drew a quick breath, cheeks pink, eyes still flashing. "Thankfully it was a false alarm. I wasn't pregnant. But it showed me who he really was, and I was crushed. I loved him. I'd thought we were going to be together forever."

"And then what happened?"

"We broke up, and I decided to take a year off, and go have an adventure. Here I am."

"Here you are," he murmured, chest tight, body aching, thinking her boyfriend had been a fool. And not just a fool, but a liar. A cheat. A scoundrel. She was right on all accounts. "How's your heart doing now?"

She smiled faintly. "Still a little banged up. But better. Stronger."

"Good." It was all he could do not to keep his hands to himself. He wanted to kiss her badly. He was hard and hungry and restless in a way he hadn't been for a very long time.

He signaled to the waiter. The waiter approached quickly. "The check?" he said to Shane.

"No. The dessert menu." Shane glanced at Jet. "Feel like dessert?" he asked, wanting her to say yes, if only to keep her in a public place, out of arm's reach and relatively safe.

"Not really," she answered. "Not unless you want something."

He did want something. But it wasn't on the menu. "Check is fine," he told the waiter, blood thrumming through his veins. He was so hard he was uncomfortable, his jeans now far too tight.

Outside, he walked her to his rented car. He unlocked the passenger side door for her and swung it open but before she could climb in, he reached for her, one hand cupping her cheek, lifting her face to his. His head dropped and his mouth brushed hers, once, and then again. Teasing. Tasting.

She was wearing a light floral scented fragrance that made him think of spring just before it turned to summer, and he breathed her in...lilacs...gardenias...something delicate and fresh...

She tasted just as fresh and sweet. He wanted more. Shane deepened the kiss, the pressure of his mouth parting her lips ever so slightly. He stroked the seam of her lips and her mouth parted wider. She gave a little sigh of pleasure as his tongue explored her mouth and he pulled her closer, an arm low on her waist, his hand in the small of her back. They were standing between patches of dirt and ice-crusted snow and yet the night blazed, hot and bright.

He held her against him, a hand tangling in her thick, glossy hair. His kiss drank her in. Her taste was intoxicating...addictive. He couldn't remember when he last wanted anyone this much.

When he finally lifted his head, she was clinging to the lapel of his coat, her blue eyes cloudy, expression dazed. "Um, wow," she whispered, dropping her hands to bury them in her coat pockets. She took a step back. "Not bad. Apparently you're quite good at a couple things."

THAT KISS.

Wow. Just uh, wow.

It'd been five minutes since he'd kissed her, *at least* five minutes, as they'd left Livingston behind and were traveling south on 89, back to Marietta.

And yet her lips still tingled. Her whole body tingled. Every little nerve seemed to be awake and dancing.

Maybe the kiss wasn't really that good.

Maybe it just seemed that good because it had been ten months since she'd last kissed anyone.

Maybe Ben was a lousy kisser and she'd forgotten that kissing could light her up like a Christmas tree.

Or maybe Shane was just damn good.

"You're awfully quiet," Shane said, breaking the silence.

"I was just trying to figure something out."

He shot her a swift glance. "And what would that be?"

She shouldn't say it. She shouldn't. "Are you that good of a kisser, or was Ben just bad?"

For a long minute Shane didn't say anything and her question just hung in the air between them. And then his hard jaw eased, and he smiled at her, the smile knowing, and more than a little wicked. "I'm just really good."

She didn't know if it was his smile or his words but she went hot all over, so hot it was like jumping into a boiling pot. "That's pretty confident."

His lips quirked. "Or honest."

She looked at him, her gaze sweeping from the top of his dark head to the length of his sinewy thighs. The man was seriously appealing. "Girls must just fall at your feet."

He didn't answer right away. "I don't have a problem meeting women, no."

"So what are your rules when you date?" She saw the lift of his brow and hurriedly added, "You know what I mean. You obviously have them, because you're thirty-something and single."

"That's because I'm married to my career. There is no time for a wife or kids."

"Do you want kids one day?"

He shot her an indecipherable look. "Not planning on a family, but having grown up bounced from place to place, I'd never do that to a kid. If I made one, I'd raise him."

He returned his attention to the highway and they drove in silence for a mile or two before Shane added, "I'm not a fan of abortion. I wouldn't dictate to anyone else. We each have our own beliefs, but for me, life is life, and it needs to be protected."

"You really mean that?" she whispered after a moment. "Or are you just saying what I want to hear?"

His laugh was low and rough. "I'm not a kiss-ass, no."

She flushed and crossed one leg over the over, thinking the inside of the Range Rover suddenly felt far too small and warm. "I didn't mean that."

"Good. Because I'd never tell someone something just because I thought it was what they'd want to hear. If you ask me something, I'll tell you the truth."

"I'm glad."

He shot her a cool glance. "Do you want to ask me something?"

She gave a tug on her seatbelt, trying to loosen it, feeling as if she couldn't breathe. "No."

"You can. Is there anything about the book, or the Sheenans—"

"No." But she'd said it fast, too fast, and they both knew it. Jet swallowed hard, gathering her thoughts, and courage. "But if something comes up, if there is something I want or need to know, I will ask. I promise."

"Good. Far better to ask, than to assume." He flashed her a smile, his hard jaw easing, his teeth white in the light of the dash, and just that quick, lazy smile made her pulse drum and her chest ache with an emotion she couldn't define.

She liked him, and she was going to have to be careful not to let herself care too much. Jet had a problem of caring too much...falling too hard. It was why she'd been avoiding dating. Better to keep men at arm's length than let one close and risk getting hurt again.

Finally the lights of Marietta glowed in the distance. "Almost there," she said.

Shane put on his signal as they approached the turn off for Marietta. "You mentioned rules earlier," he said, braking for the off ramp. "And I guess I do have them. In my world, a man never turns his back on his woman, or his child. Ever. So if you want rules, those are mine. Other than that, everything else is negotiable."

And then they were on Bramble, passing the high school, traveling the dark street to Kara's.

Pulling up in front of Kara's yellow house, Jet saw that the front porch light was on, and more lights shone from the inside. Kara must still be up.

"Here we are," Jet said, reaching for the seatbelt buckle.

Shane shifted into park. "I'll walk you to the door."

"You don't have to. It's right there. I'm not—"

But he turned the engine off, and swung the door open and stepped out, ignoring whatever else she was going to say.

Jet frowned as his door slammed shut. She swung her door open, not about to sit and wait. She didn't do helpless.

She hadn't been raised to be dependent. "Thank you for dinner," she said crisply, meeting him on the pavement. "I had a great time."

"Thank you for joining me," he replied, matching her formal tone before his hard jaw eased and he flashed a crooked smile. He walked with her towards the porch. "I just hope it won't get you into too much trouble with the Sheenans."

The sidewalk was narrow and her shoulder brushed his chest as they walked. "It's fine. Don't worry." She was so conscious of him there, next to her, as she reached into her purse, fumbling for the key. "Good luck with your book. I can't wait to read it."

"Is that it?" he asked, his voice husky, as if amused. "This is goodbye?"

"Well, you never know...we're both busy. I might not see you again."

"Marietta has a population of eleven thousand—if that. It's kind of hard not to bump into people here."

She flushed and hoped it was dark enough that he couldn't see. "That's true. Our paths will probably pass. Again. Sometime."

"Or, we don't wait for our paths to cross, and we make a plan. Set a date. Say for brunch on Sunday? I've been told the Graff does a very nice Sunday brunch."

Her pulse jumped. The Graff, being the Graff Hotel, also known as Troy Sheenan's hotel. He'd bought the abandoned turn-of-the-century hotel and spent a decade restoring it. Today it was the finest four-star hotel between Three Forks and Yellowstone but it was also a place that she probably shouldn't go with Shane. "I usually go to church with Harley and the kids on Sunday. It's kind of our tradition."

"Brock doesn't go?"

"The Sheenans aren't big on attending services, but they say a blessing at dinner, and prayers with the kids." She looked up at him. "Do you attend church?"

"No."

"I guess you fit right in then."

"Except that I'm not a Sheenan," he retorted.

"Obviously. I didn't mean that. I just meant—" She struggled to find the right words, and then shrugged. "Never mind. Doesn't matter."

"So no to brunch," he said.

"If we care about what others think," she said.

"I don't care, but I know you do, and I respect that." He reached into his coat pocket and withdrew his car keys. "I'll see you when I see you. If not at the diner then maybe at Java Cafe."

Disappointment flooded her. His tone was kind. His words had been kind. He'd said nothing offensive and yet her heart just fell, toppling all the way down. She didn't want to wait days, or weeks, to see him again. She didn't want to leave everything so open ended.

She'd loved tonight. Even the uncomfortable and awkward parts.

"I've never been to the Graff to eat," she said hesitantly, feeling her way through this. "I've had a drink in their lounge, and I understand at Christmas they do this festive holiday tea on weekends, and a Santa Brunch a week or two before Christmas—" She broke off, gulped air. "Do you think it's terrible that I want to go to brunch with you?"

"No. But I don't think you're someone who can handle disappointing her family."

"We're not getting married. We'd be having brunch."

"This is true."

She looked away, frowned as she remembered how upset Cormac had been tonight. If he didn't like her having dinner with Shane in Livingston, he definitely wouldn't like her meeting Shane for brunch at the Graff. But Cormac wasn't her brother or her father, and he wasn't the easiest of men, either. He had a stubborn streak a mile long and tended to do what he wanted to do…regardless.

"The hotel's history is fascinating," she said after a moment. She turned her attention back to Shane. "Do you know it?"

"A little. I stayed there for a few days when I first arrived in town. Met Dillon Sheenan in the hotel bar for lunch to discuss leasing the Sheenan place. The bar was nice. It looked like a pub, very masculine but stylish."

"The entire hotel was recently renovated."

"I understand it stood empty for years before the renovation."

She nodded. "Troy bought it because it was his mom's favorite place. His mother used to take her little boys there for special events, back before the hotel went out of business."

"I didn't know that."

"Harley told me the hotel nearly bankrupted Troy, too. It was a huge multi-million dollar renovation but Troy believed in the hotel and I think it's out of the red now. I hope it's out of the red."

"You're full of information."

She grinned crookedly. "You can't help picking up bits and pieces of history when you're here. My students are proud to be Montanans. Most of them love living in Paradise Valley and intend to make their homes here, too." She shivered at a blast of icy wind. "I have to say, though, it's cold here. Really cold. And that wind that whistles through the valley from Yellowstone. Brrr."

"Let's get you inside then." He walked her up the steps of the porch. "So, eleven on Sunday? Or should we try for noon so you can attend church fist?"

"Noon would be great."

"I'll pick you up."

"Maybe I'll meet you there." She made a face. "Just safer."

"So the Sheenans won't like you seeing me."

"Um, no," she admitted. "They won't."

"Then maybe we shouldn't. I don't want everyone upset with you. It's not fair to you—"

"Or you," she countered. "And I wouldn't go if I thought I was hurting anyone, but I'm not. This isn't about them. So, from a purely selfish standpoint, I want to go to brunch. I like your company and, you know, you're the first person—outside of Kara and my family—who has reached out to me here, or included me. So really, you're the first friend I've made in Marietta, and after five weeks, it feels good to be making friends." She searched his face, wishing the porch light was brighter, wanting to better see what he was thinking, but the light illuminated just his jaw and mouth, leaving his dark eyes shadowed. "You know?"

He studied her for a moment, his lips firm and unsmiling, and then he nodded slowly. "I do," he said quietly.

And then he leaned towards her and pressed a light kiss to her forehead, and then another light kiss to her lips, before letting her go. "Sleep well."

"You, too," she murmured, heart thudding hard, before unlocking the front door and slipping inside.

She liked him. Really liked him. And this was going to be a problem.

Kara was awake, waiting for Jet in the living room, watching TV, a glowing fire in the hearth, when Jet arrived home at eleven-thirty. Jet shot Kara a worried look as she peeled off her gloves and then her coat. "What's wrong?"

Kara turned off the TV. "Your sister was here earlier. She waited for you for almost an hour. You didn't have your phone on you, did you?"

"No. I left it charging and forgot it. What's wrong? Did something happen to one of the kids?"

"No. It just seems like your whole family knows you had dinner with Shane and they're not happy."

"The Diekerhofs?"

Kara gave her a look as if to say Jet was being deliberately dense. "No, the Sheenans."

Jet sighed. "The Sheenans aren't my family. They're Harley's." She laid her coat and gloves on the back of the couch and came around to sit on the opposite end of Kara. "And if Cormac had to go tell everyone…well, that's rather sad."

"The Sheenans are really upset about the book."

"I gather. But why be so protective of McKenna? I've met her. She doesn't strike me as all that fragile."

"It's not that she's fragile, but there's concern that a lot of money will be made off of a tragedy, and none of the money benefits the victims—"

"The Sheenans want a piece of the book?"

"No. They don't want it written at all. They don't want anyone to capitalize on the murders." Kara rose and took a poker to the glowing embers, spreading them out. "It's a sordid piece of Marietta history, and no one here wants to see it exploited. And beyond the financial side, it was truly a terrible time, with everyone under the microscope, and no one more closely than the Sheenans."

"Why the Sheenans?"

Kara sat back down and drew her legs up under her. "The Douglases and Sheenans were neighbors. They shared a property line. In fact, you had to drive on the Sheenan ranch to get to the Douglas', so whoever the killer was, he'd been on the Sheenan property, too. So when Rory went for help, he went to the Sheenans. Brock and Bill raced to the Douglas house, while one of the other boys summoned help."

"Brock and Mr. Sheenan were the first on the scene?"

Kara nodded. "Another neighbor, rancher Rob MacCredie, was next, and then the sheriff, fire, and ambulances. But because Bill and Brock were first on the scene, they were questioned again and again—"

"There is no way Brock was part of that."

"Of course not. But he saw it all, and an investigation always zeros in on family and neighbors. No one escapes unscathed." She was silent a moment. "I was only six or seven at the time, but I remember how tense everyone was. How *scared*. No one felt safe anymore. It honestly took years for people to feel comfortable in their own homes."

"Were any of the Douglas kids in your class?"

"I was the same age as one of the boys that died, but he went to your school, in Paradise Valley, and I attended Marietta Elementary."

Jet couldn't even imagine how terrifying it'd be to discover that a child your own age had been murdered in his home, and that the parents couldn't even protect him. That the parents had been killed, too.

"Why do you think Shane wanted to rent the Sheenan house?" she asked Kara.

"It's convenient. It's right there where everything happened." Kara rose and stretched. "But just because something is convenient, doesn't make it right. Not when something has caused so much suffering in this community."

"I would think the community would want justice for the Douglases."

"I don't think that anyone really believes the crime can be solved. It's been too many years. The evidence—" She broke off, sighed. "Listen, I became a district attorney because I couldn't stand to think that bad guys got to get away unpunished. The bad guys should be held accountable. My entire career is based on righting wrongs, but in this case, there is no identifiable bad guy, and I don't think there ever will be." She covered a yawn. "I've got to go to bed. I'm heading to Billings tomorrow to see my grandmother, but *please* call your sister in the morning. I don't want her thinking I didn't tell you, and Harley is pretty anxious about talking to you."

All the more reason Jet wasn't looking forward to the call. "I'll call her. I'll phone after breakfast. I promise."

But once in her room, Jet didn't want to think about Harley or the Sheenans or the horrific murders on the

Douglas ranch. She wanted to think about Shane, and the kiss, and how he made her feel...

Of how she felt right now.

Ben had crushed her and she'd thought she wasn't ready for anything but somehow, inexplicably, she found herself hoping...

Hoping Shane might like her a little bit.

Hoping he'd want to see more of her, not just Sunday, but after Sunday.

Hoping she could get Harley and Cormac and the rest of the Sheenans to respect her friendship with Shane, because really, that was all it was right now.

Yes, he made her feel all excited and fizzy on the inside, but at the same time, she didn't want romance without a real friendship. Friendship was important. If her breakup with Ben had taught her anything it was she couldn't have a relationship without honesty and respect and communication.

Changing into her pajamas, she washed her face and then brushed her teeth and climbed into bed.

Tomorrow she'd call Harley and then would go to school and prepare her lessons for the coming week and then Sunday would be brunch...

A little quiver of excitement shot through her. She smiled in the dark.

She shouldn't like him this much. She shouldn't.

But he was so fascinating...absolutely larger than life. He

wasn't just ruggedly handsome and intellectually stimulating, but he had a smoldering intensity, which she'd never encountered before, and a sizzling intensity made her so curious.

She wanted to understand the attraction. She wanted to understand *him*.

Who was Sean Shane Swan Finley? And why did his parents change his name on the birth certificate? And who was the beautiful mother that used to visit him and then vanished so abruptly from his life?

Chapter Five

S HANE HAD WAITED outside the small, yellow house until Jet was safely inside. He'd watched the front door until the porch light was turned off and only then did he return to his truck, start the engine, and pull away from the curb.

At the corner he flipped a U-turn and headed back down Bramble to pick up Highway 89 north of the high school.

It'd take him at least twenty minutes to get to the Sheenan ranch, and he drove slowly, mindful of the black ice on the road. He was in no great hurry to return to the old two-story log cabin. The old Sheenan homestead wasn't his home, and the longer he was there, the more uncomfortable he became.

He did not belong.

He wasn't supposed to be there.

His certainty had little to do with Cormac and the other Sheenan brothers, but the heaviness that filled him every time he entered the house.

He hadn't believed in spirits before he moved in. He did now.

He was most definitely not alone in the house. His

mother's ghost—sad but benign—and another one, far more aggressive. He wouldn't be surprised if it was his father's spirit as it seemed to go out of its way to make him feel unwelcome, reminding Shane he didn't belong. That he'd never belonged. And yet whenever he felt the hostile presence, the other one was there, too, as if trying to be a buffer, determined to protect Shane.

God, he'd love to know the truth.

Why was he given away? Why had his father's name been stripped from the birth certificate—because Bill Sheenan was his father, the DNA test four years ago proved it—but Shane had waited too long to confront his father? Bill Sheenan was dead. The brothers had all abandoned the family homestead. And now Shane was here, still the outsider, still the interloper.

Shane hadn't expected a warm welcome from the Sheenan brothers, but he had thought maybe—and now he could see how silly he'd been—just maybe, they'd help him. He'd thought they'd be civil, possibly friendly. He'd thought he could get them to trust him and sit down and talk to him about what had happened leading up to the massacre on the Douglas property.

Before signing the lease, he'd hoped he'd get to know these brothers, not as brothers, but as people. Men. There was no need for a big, bonding thing, and no need to become close as they'd never be a family, but he hadn't anticipated the freeze-out.

To be fair, Dillon had been friendly enough when Shane had talked to him about leasing the house. He'd enjoyed their lunch at the Graff. Dillon had been somewhat guarded and Shane hadn't known if that was just Dillon's personality or a family thing. Nine months later Shane knew it was a family thing.

There was nothing soft about the Sheenans. They'd obviously been raised with a firm hand...taught from birth what it meant to be a Sheenan, and a man.

More than once Shane had tried to imagine growing up in that house, as a Sheenan. In terms of the lineup, he would have been near the end, sandwiched between Cormac and Dillon.

His birth date was less than a year after Cormac. He and Cormac were Irish twins, with Cormac's birthday on April fifth, while Shane's was fast approaching, February twenty-seventh. Cormac would have been just a couple months old when their mother conceived again.

Shane had wondered if that might have been part of the problem, if there had just been too many babies too quickly. Perhaps the family had been having some kind of financial difficulty or his mother had been ill, necessitating the need for her mother to step in and help take care of the new baby.

So odd to think of how it might have been, the lineup and pecking order—Brock, Troy, Trey, Cormac, Shane, and then Dillon.

For the first two weeks of his life, he'd been a Sheenan,

and then mid-March the birth certificate was amended and he became a Swan.

Bill Sheenan was not crazy. He was a tough man but smart, successful, and respected by all but neighbor Hawksley Carrigan.

Why would he remove his name from the birth certificate?

For him to do that, he had to be sure that Shane wasn't his.

Except Bill Sheenan was wrong. The private investigator Shane had hired four years ago had been able to run a DNA test off a Starbucks coffee cup that Troy discarded after a meeting with a potential investor—Shane's investigator—and Troy was a ninety-nine percent match for a sibling, which meant Shane was as much a Sheenan as Trey and Troy, since they were identical twins.

Arriving at the ranch, Shane parked in the gravel area between the house and barn and headed for the two-story log cabin.

He discovered a white envelope tacked to the wooden front door.

Cormac, he thought. Cormac had put the notice in writing.

Shane removed the envelope, unlocked the door and stepped inside to read the paper. He'd been right. Thirty-day notice. In writing.

For a moment Shane didn't know what to think. He'd

been expecting this for awhile but, now that it had come, he was numb.

These past nine months hadn't been easy or comfortable. But what had he hoped? That living in his parents' house would heal something inside of him? That sleeping in his brother's bed would knit that gaping hole in his heart?

Irritated and frustrated, he walked through the house, flipping switches until the entire downstairs blazed with light. But it wasn't enough. The house seemed to be listening, waiting for something, and Shane synced his phone with his Bluetooth speakers, filling the house with Aerosmith, upping the volume until the glass figurines in the dining room's china cabinet rattled. Nothing like a good, old 1973 classic to wake the house up. And the ghosts...if they were sleeping.

Did ghosts sleep?

Sing for the laughter...

Shane had been born in 1982—at least that was what his grandmother claimed—but he loved seventies rock, not the disco stuff sweeping Europe and the US, but rock with all its genres...punk, glam, hard, progressive, art, heavy metal. But, by far, hard rock was his favorite and his iPod had been filled with Deep Purple, Led Zeppelin, Queen, Black Sabbath, AC/DC, Kiss, Aerosmith, Van Halen, and more.

Whenever there was friction in one of the homes, the music was always blared.

The ultra-conservative far right folks would warn that he

was going to hell, and complain to the agency that Shane was always listening to satanic music.

Shane would just put on headphones and turn the volume louder.

Knowing no one was within ten miles of the cabin, Shane turned the speakers all the way up now, the music blasting through the house.

Sing for the tears...

He drummed his hand against his thigh as he walked from room to room, circling the downstairs, kitchen to hall, hall through the dining room, dining room to the entry, past the stairs and into the living room.

Standing in the living room, he faced the neat built-in bookcases that framed the lower half of the fireplace. The shelves held maybe a dozen books total, one of them an old dictionary, and the other, an even older Bible.

He took the Bible from the shelf, the black leather scuffed and cracked, and flipped through the tissue thin, gilt-edged pages. Here and there select passages were delicately underlined in pencil. A church program was tucked in the New Testament, in John. Shane wondered if it was there by chance, or if someone had left it there deliberately. A bookmark perhaps. He opened the book more fully, inspecting the pages. More light pencil marks quoted a passage from John 4:16: *And we have known and believed the love that God hath to us. God is love; and he that dwelleth in love dwelleth in God, and God in him.*

Steven Tyler's voice rose in the background. *Dream on...*

Shane closed the book, unable to read scripture in King James English with Tyler's piercing wail filling the air.

Dream on, indeed.

JET FELL ASLEEP feeling strong and brave and more than a little bit defiant. But when she woke, her first thought was, *oh, no...Harley*.

She had to call Harley soon and it wasn't a call Jet wanted to make.

Dragging herself from bed, she opened the curtain and glanced up at the sky. The sun was shining, and during the night the gusting wind had blown the storm clouds away, leaving the winter sky a vivid blue. It looked like a gorgeous day, a gorgeous, *cold* day, since the blanket of clouds had kept temperatures warmer.

Jet had planned to go to the schoolhouse after breakfast to change her bulletin boards and prepare lessons for the week, but the school would be freezing—the school board turned off the heat on the weekends—and Jet dreaded the layers she'd have to put on to get through the morning there.

Fortunately, Kara kept her house warm and, even better, she'd left coffee warming in the kitchen. *Bless her*, Jet thought, as she filled her mug and then topped off the coffee with creamer before glancing out the kitchen window towards the driveway.

Kara's car was gone, already on the road to Billings,

which meant Jet had the house to herself all day. Nice.

Jet grabbed the paper from the kitchen table, carried it into the living room, and curled up on the couch to read and savor her coffee.

She was still on the front page when her phone rang minutes later. Jet's heart sank, certain it was Harley.

She dashed to the bedroom and retrieved her phone from where it was still charging. "Morning," she greeted her sister.

"Glad you answered. I was beginning to think you were avoiding me," Harley said crisply.

"Not avoiding you. I just woke up."

"I texted you earlier."

"I literally woke up ten, fifteen minutes ago. Haven't even gotten through my first cup of coffee yet, and you know how much I love my coffee."

"But you never sleep this late."

"Because I have to be at school early every day, but its Saturday. The weekend." Jet sat down again on the couch, and grabbed the blue, crocheted afghan from the back of the couch, spreading it over her lap. "What's up?"

"You know what's up." Harley sighed. "I'm sure Kara talked to you last night. And I know you spoke to Cormac last night, too."

Jet sipped her coffee, letting her sister talk.

"And you know how everyone feels about him," Harley added. "He's got everyone in the family upset."

"But he's not writing an expose, Harley. And he's not a

hack. He's one of the most talented, respected writers alive. His books are works of art—"

"Maybe, but this particular book will cause tremendous pain. It's already stirring everyone up. Brock is really unhappy about it, and there isn't a lot that bothers him. You know that."

"But what if Shane's able to help solve the crime? Wouldn't McKenna and her family want that?"

"It's been eighteen years since the home invasion. The case is cold."

"Shane thinks he knows what happened."

Harley was silent for a long time. When she spoke again her voice was pitched low. "The Sheenans do *not* approve of him profiting from the Douglas' loss. He will make a fortune, Jet. It's selfish and exploitive and it just feeds people's insatiable hunger—"

"He's not writing a sensationalized version of a crime. That's not the kind of books he writes."

"How do you know?"

"Because I've read his books. All six of them. He's an award-winning writer, and an honest, respected researcher. I trust him."

"The Sheenans don't."

"Why not?"

"He was sneaky. He should have told them what he was writing when he asked to lease the house. But he didn't, because he knew they would say no."

"That's probably why he didn't tell them."

"Are you defending him?"

"I'm saying there are two sides to every story—"

"You are not taking his side, Jet!"

"I'm not taking sides. I just don't agree that it's necessary to escalate this. He won't be here forever—"

"You can't go out with him again," Harley interrupted, her voice cool and sharp.

Jet pulled the phone from her ear and stared at it a moment, shocked. *Did Harley really just say that?*

When Jet didn't immediately answer Harley cleared her throat, adding a little more gently, "Are you there, Jet?"

"Yes, I'm here. And I heard what you said, but no."

"No?"

"Yes, no. I don't agree. I'm not agreeing, and I'm not going to cold shoulder him just because the Sheenans don't like the book he's writing."

"This man can't be that important to you after one date!"

"It wasn't even a date. It was just dinner."

"So it shouldn't be an issue."

"Then don't make it one, Harley."

There was a long pause on the other end of the line. Jet could feel the tension humming between them. Jet never argued with Harley. But Harley was usually reasonable. Levelheaded.

"Would it make more sense if McKenna explains it to you?" Harley asked after another tense beat of silence.

"Would you understand how sensitive this is if she were to share her perspective?"

Jet couldn't imagine putting McKenna through that. "No."

"Or Trey can explain—"

"*No*." Jet shuddered. Trey was intense and fiercely protective of McKenna and the last thing Jet needed was a little chat with Trey. "And Brock doesn't have to, either," she added hastily. "I understand what you're saying, and it's not necessary to threaten me with *your* family."

"Now you're being silly. I'm not threatening you. I'm trying to make you understand how traumatic this is for all of them. You and I weren't here when it took place, and it's just a story to us, but they lived through this. Jet, McKenna lost her family. Her mom and dad. Her three younger siblings. The baby, Grace, was just two. And they were all killed. *Violently*."

Jet closed her eyes, trying to block the pictures Harley was putting in her head. "I don't know that much about what happened," she admitted.

"Well, maybe you should find out. Maybe if you did a little research you'd understand why everyone wants to protect McKenna and her bothers from more pain."

Jet didn't answer, too busy trying to process everything her sister was saying.

Harley waited, and then asked quietly, "So you'll keep your distance from Shane? No more dates? No more coffee chats?"

Jet's heart sank. What all did Harley know? "Coffee chats?"

"Taylor saw you with Shane at Java Café Wednesday afternoon. You were having coffee together—"

"He needed a place to sit until a table opened up." Jet battled her frustration. She'd grown up in a small town, but Marietta was ridiculous. "We talked *briefly*."

"Is that when he asked you to dinner?"

"*Harley*."

"I'm not trying to make waves, Jet. I'm trying to protect you. I promise. This could get ugly and I don't want you in the middle."

Jet silently counted to five, and then exhaled. "Got it."

"So you'll stay away from Shane?"

"We're having brunch tomorrow at the Graff."

"Cancel it."

Jet counted to ten this time. "I can't do that. It's not fair to Shane."

"And how is it fair to the Sheenans that you're having brunch with Shane at the Graff? It's going to be a slap in their face. It's the family hotel. And Shane knows that. That's why he's taking you there. He's using you, Jet. Can't you see that?"

When Jet didn't answer, Harley's voice dropped. "Have I ever lied to you, Jet? Have I ever deceived you in any way?"

"No," Jet whispered.

"No. And I wouldn't. Because you're my sister. And family is the most important thing in the world to me. I'd never lie to you. Do you believe me?"

Jet closed her eyes, squeezing them shut, holding the air in for a moment before she exhaled. "Yes, I believe you care about me," she said quietly, because she did.

Harley might be a bossy, big sister but Harley always put family first. "But I don't think Shane is using me." And then she hung up.

After ending the call, Jet sat motionless on the couch, coffee and paper forgotten.

She'd told Harley that Shane wouldn't use her, but honestly, she wasn't sure, not anymore. Not after Harley had planted the seeds of doubt.

If Jet was being honest, Shane was way out of her league, and had been out of her league from the moment they'd met.

She hadn't thought of dinner as a date. They were going out for a meal, two acquaintances, not yet friends. But then, leaving dinner, he'd kissed her and the kiss was so good and so hot, bone meltingly hot, that she'd lost all perspective.

Had the kiss fogged her brain? Was she being blinded to what was happening in front of her?

And yet when she thought about the kiss, it made her feel fizzy all over again. On paper, a thirty-four-year old, internationally acclaimed writer and twenty-four-year old teacher should have little in common, but when they were together it felt right. It felt natural and interesting and exciting.

The kiss had been exciting. It made her hope for things, and feel things...

Jet reached for her mug and clasped it to her chest, her hands tight around the ceramic, letting the heat warm her, as she tried to wade through Harley's argument. Harley was always good at presenting facts. She was the logical, pragmatic Diekerhof. Jet was the passionate, adventurous one.

But being passionate and adventurous did get her into trouble sometimes.

Was Shane using her?

She tried hard to see it, she did, but when she remembered how she felt last night at dinner, and how she felt when he kissed her goodnight, she didn't feel used. She felt connected to Shane. Protective, even.

She didn't see him anymore as this big New York writer with the fancy website and the movie deals. To her, he was Shane Swan, the boy who'd been raised on a reservation near Flathead Lake before being put into foster care.

But if Harley was outraged and Brock was upset and sides were being drawn, Jet couldn't risk alienating her sister and her sister's new family.

Blinking, Jet cleared the salty sting in her eyes and reached for her phone. She sent Shane a quick text. *Something came up. Can't meet for brunch. Good luck with your book. Jet*

And then before she could cry, she grabbed her coffee,

headed to the bathroom, and turned on the shower and stepped beneath the spray while it was still cold. The chill shocked her and shivering she turned in a slow circle, letting the icy water pelt down, using the cold to stiffen her resolve. She wasn't going to cry over another guy. She wasn't going to be that girl. She wasn't going to be a weak, blubbering, overly emotional girl who needed a guy to be happy.

She didn't need a man. She was having an adventure. *Just think of everything she was getting to do—teach in a historic one room schoolhouse, work in stunning Paradise Valley, live in a sleepy little former mining town.* How cool was that?

Shivering, she did another circle beneath the spray. She was lucky to be here, lucky to have a sister that loved her. There was no reason to let one date with some guy—even if he was a seriously smart, sexy, fascinating guy—turn her world inside out.

Teeth chattering, she turned off the shower, grabbed a towel and dried off.

Leaving the bathroom, she grabbed her coffee and phone. She glanced down at the phone as she hustled back to her bedroom and spotted a message from Shane.

Which Sheenan called you this morning? I got Cormac.

Jet read the message a second time as she yanked faded jeans on over underwear that stuck to her still damp skin. She hooked her bra and then pulled on a gray T-shirt and a thick wine-colored sweater over that.

She dragged her hair into a ponytail, high on the back of

her head, before answering Shane. *Harley called me,* She typed, before hitting send.

That's good. I can't imagine her promising to beat the living daylight out of you, came the reply.

Jet stilled. Her hand shook ever so slightly as she typed. *Cormac said that?*

I'm not worried. As long as you're okay, that's my main concern.

She was worried. She typed quickly. *I can't believe he'd threaten you!*

I'm not scared of Cormac, or any of them. I just don't want you getting dragged into the middle of this. It's not your fight. So I agree Sunday is a bad idea. Just know if you ever need anything, I'm here.

He was letting her go, saying goodbye.

Jet pressed a fist to her mouth and held her breath, telling herself she should be relieved that he was closing the door and pushing her away, but she didn't feel relieved. She felt wildly conflicted.

Still holding her breath she typed one last message. *Harley said you were using me to get close to the Sheenans. Was that true?*

She waited for him to answer, wondering if he would. A few moments later the little dots appeared, indicating he was typing a response.

Yes, he said.

He sent a follow up text almost immediately. *I'd hoped you could introduce me to Brock. I thought maybe he'd be willing to meet with me if you put in a good word for me.*

Jet exhaled slowly, disappointed, and hurt. So he did want something from her. Harley had been right. *You should have told me.*

I was going to talk to you tomorrow at brunch.

Jet stared at the last message for a long minute before writing. *And the kiss?*

That was because you're beautiful.

JET SPENT THE day at the schoolhouse, taking down old bulletin boards and putting up new ones that reflected February education themes—President's Day, Black History Month, Inventors & Inventions, the ocean, and then, just because it was pretty and fun, Valentine's Day hearts here and there.

As she stapled and pinned, she tried not to think about Shane but it was virtually impossible. Decorating bulletin boards might keep her hands busy but it left her thoughts free. And so she thought about Shane, and the Sheenans, and how awful the conflict was between them. There was no reason for it to get to this point. No reason for Cormac to threaten Shane in any way. That had to be the most childish thing she'd ever heard.

She also hated how the Sheenans were ganging up on Shane. He was one person and they were a big and formidable group. She understood why the Sheenans weren't happy about the book, but Shane didn't owe them anything. He could write about whatever he wanted.

Jet climbed up her stepladder to tack a huge paper cutout of George Washington's head on one end of the bulletin board, running above the old, black chalkboard, and then carried the ladder and pins to the other end where she added Abraham Lincoln's head.

It was a shame, she thought, that none of the Sheenans had tried to get to know Shane. Maybe if they'd been willing to talk to him about the book, and share their knowledge and memories, they'd get a better sense of the scope of the book as well as Shane's intentions.

Climbing back down from the ladder, she stepped back to view her work. The two big paper heads against rose red paper looked like something that might have been in the classroom when she was a girl. Was that good or bad? Well, it was a change from January's blue and white color scheme at any rate. It'd have to do.

She folded the ladder up, and leaned it against the door to the back room which was a combination storage and teacher break room. Not that she went in there when the kids were present, but it had a small sink and a mini refrigerator and she'd added a microwave so she could heat up soup for her lunch.

She microwaved a bowl of tomato soup now and stared out the small window at the playground with the old set of swings. Behind the playground was a field, now covered in snow.

This was such a small school, in such a small town, and yet suddenly she felt overwhelmed by problems that weren't her own.

SHANE WAS SUPPOSED to be writing. He was behind on the book. More behind than he'd ever been. If he didn't make significant progress quickly, there would be no way to get the book in on time.

And he kind of didn't care.

No, not true. He cared about being late, his reputation mattered, but he hated this book. He didn't like anything about it, and he'd only tackled the subject because it had been an excuse to come to Marietta and live amongst the Sheenans and pretend he was working on something when, all along, all he wanted was to know who these people were. And why they didn't want him.

Hell and damnation.

Shane threw his pen across the room and it hit one of the bulletin boards before falling to the floor.

Of course the book would be easier to write if he had a definitive idea about who committed the crime—and he was getting there, little by little—but time was running short and he needed to focus and he couldn't seem to make himself focus because he just didn't care.

Not because the murders didn't deserve to be solved, but because every aspect of the story was vile and heartbreaking. There was nothing good about the story. There was no lesson to be learned.

Shane left his chair and paced the dining room before stalking to the bulletin boards with the shocking headlines.

His gaze swept the headlines and then dropped to the story with the black and white photos of those who'd been slain. Todd. Grace. Gordon. Ty. Baby Grace.

Dad, Mom, a nine-year-old, a five-year-old, and a two-year-old.

They deserved better, and this book would certainly not help or heal, in any way. Life was unjust. Life was brutal. He wanted to punch something, hit something, break something—

Shane returned to his chair, his hand clenched into a fist. He squeezed until his hand ached and then he opened his laptop and sent his agent a brief email. *Mark, I want to buy the book back. I'm happy to write something else, something on Montana history, but I'll need more time. It's impossible to write something new for an April 30th deadline.*

Shane hit send and closed his laptop. Leaning back in his chair he looked at the bulletin boards with the newspaper headlines and articles. They disgusted him. The senseless violence. The heartbreaking waste of life. He knew the police reports. He'd read the reports from the coroner's office and knew how each of them had died. He'd discovered that Mrs. Douglas had been sexually assaulted at some point during the attack. He'd read that Mr. Douglas was probably still alive at that point.

There were nights Shane couldn't sleep because he couldn't get the horror out of his head. He could imagine the children's tears and terror. He could almost feel Mr. Douglas' helplessness and hopelessness as his family was tortured in front of him.

Shane's phone rang. He grimaced, recognizing his agent's cell. "Mark," he said, answering.

"Got your email."

"Hate to bother you on a weekend."

"Glad you emailed. What's going on?"

"You saw my email. I'm not going to finish this one, it's not right, it's not what anyone needs."

"Everyone needs this one. Everyone loves this one. You've got a film deal and foreign sales out the kazoo. A massive print run. Publicity like you wouldn't believe—"

"It's wrong. It's making me sick."

"Maybe you're too close. Maybe you need a break. Get in your car and drive. Clear your head, get some perspective."

"It won't help. I'm not going to write it—"

"Shane, hey bud, relax, it's all okay, it's going to be okay. I can buy you more time. That's not a problem. I'll tell them you just need some extra time."

"It's the subject, not the issue of time."

"Deadlines can be stressful."

"You're not listening, Mark—"

"I'm listening," his agent interrupted quietly, "but

Shane, you have to finish this. You were paid a huge advance for this, half of it has already been deposited into your account."

"I'll return it."

"And what about my percentage? I've spent my piece. And the piece coming. I have kids in college. You're putting my daughter through Princeton and my son through Columbia. Their tuition is funded by you. And my little girl, the one in junior high? The dancer? Her dance team travels and competes because you write these books that allow me to underwrite her team. You pay our bills."

"You'd handled six other books—"

"And I've spent that money, too."

"What about your other authors?"

"Shane, no one is as big as you. You're my star. You're my business."

Shane closed his eyes and held his breath, trying to see a way through. There had to be some kind of option here.

"Drive to White Fish," Mark said with forced cheer. "Ski. Get fresh air. You'll feel better. You've got cabin fever, and it's natural. You're at that point of the book. It happens with every book."

Shane didn't speak.

"Shane, buddy, listen to me. You've never not met a deadline. Never. Ever. In ten years you've never once been late on anything. You'll come through. You'll be fine."

"It's different this time."

Mark was silent a moment. "How different?"

"Career changing different."

"Don't say that. Don't ever say that again. You're brilliant. Your books are works of art—"

"I don't need the bullshit."

"It's not. You're huge. And not just for me, but for the publisher. You make them a lot of money."

"I don't mind when it's the right story. This is the wrong one."

Silence stretched across the line. Finally, Mark said, "How much time do you need to make it work?"

Shane didn't answer.

Mark sighed deeply. "I'll let Saul know. We'll get you an extension. It's not a big deal. Don't put more pressure on yourself. It's not going to help. The book will be done when it's done, and that's fine."

Mark hung up.

Shane sat back in his chair and looked at the newspaper headlines and thought about how it must have been for Rory returning from dropping his sister off at a play date to find his family slain.

It must have been hell.

It must have been because it was hell trying to recreate it.

IT WAS LATE afternoon when Jet finally finished in the schoolhouse and the sky was darkening as she made her way to her car. But, reaching her vehicle, she discovered that one of the doors was slightly ajar and she prayed the open door hadn't drained her battery. It'd happened once already. It seemed she had a bad habit of doing too many things at one time, resulting in interior car lights being left on, or the hatchback door slightly open.

Climbing behind the wheel she tried to start the car, but it made a feeble dying sound before going silent.

She grimaced. So not good. There was no way she wanted to call Harley and Brock now.

She pumped the gas and tried the engine again.

Nothing.

Jet sat for a moment in the dark. The moon shone overhead. Thank goodness it wasn't snowing, but it was cold, and there wasn't a lot of traffic on this side road on a Saturday.

Why didn't she go home a couple hours ago and finish grading there? Why had she insisted on staying until every grade had been recorded?

So frustrating.

She'd have to call Harley. Good Lord, she dreaded that call.

Reaching for her phone she tapped messages, scrolling through her recent message to Harley's text from early this morning. She passed Shane's name and paused.

He was out here, up one of these roads. He couldn't be that far, either. Five or ten minutes at the most.

If he was home.

If he was willing to help her.

He'd be willing to help her.

Jet called him. He answered promptly. "Shane, here."

"Hey, it's Jet. Are you home right now?"

"Yes."

"Do you have jumper cables? I'm at school and my car battery is dead."

"Where exactly are you?"

"Take the exit on Highway 89 just before Emigrant Gulch, turn left, follow Yellowstone River up a quarter of a mile and you'll see the little schoolhouse."

"I'm leaving now, but keep your phone handy in case I need more directions."

Jet hung up, clapped her hands together, and then tucked them into her coat pockets. Harley wouldn't be happy that Shane was coming to help her, but Jet was glad. He was close. He'd be quick. And best of all, he wouldn't give her a hard time.

Chapter Six

JET'S DIRECTIONS WERE pretty good. In the deepening twilight, Shane spotted the faded red cupola, where a bell must have once hung, topped with a flagpole, minus a flag first, and only spotted Jet standing by her car as he rounded the bend in the road, the road built to accommodate the powerful Yellowstone River, his headlights illuminating her where she stood in front of the school next to her car.

She waved at him as he turned into the small gravel parking lot, and just seeing her, and that quick smile and happy wave gave him a little pang. The good kind and some of the tension he'd been feeling all day eased.

She looked cold but cute in her coat and cap and mittens. It was good to see her. She was little, but fierce, and as he slowed and pulled in front of her car, parking hood to hood to better jump her battery, he flashed back to last night, seeing Jet at the dinner table after his run-in with Cormac. She'd stared him down with her fierce teacher glare, so very, very disapproving, and he found himself smiling ruefully. He liked that she'd go toe to toe with him, holding her own, asking him questions, expecting a straight answer.

He turned off the engine, but left his headlights on as he climbed out. "Hello, trouble maker."

She laughed and walked towards him, closing the distance. "Calamity Jane. I know. That's why I couldn't call Harley."

Shane wrapped an arm around her, giving her a quick hug. "You're freezing," he said.

"Not too bad. But I am glad to see you."

"Why didn't you wait in the school?"

"I was worried you wouldn't find me. It's hard in the dark."

"I'd find you anywhere. Don't ever worry about that." His gaze met hers and held. "Now pop your hood, let's get you up and running."

While Jet unlatched her hood, he grabbed cables that had come with his rental SUV. When he'd first left college he'd bought a lemon of a car that barely ran and every couple of days he had to jumpstart the damn thing so he made quick work of hooking up the cables to the batteries now.

Once they were attached, he started his car, and then told her to start hers.

It took only one adjustment of the clips before her car started right up. "That's still a good battery," he said. "By the time you drive home, it should be charged. I wouldn't turn it off until you get home, though. Were you planning on making any stops?"

"Not now," she answered, clapping her gloved hands,

warming them. "Thank you so much. You saved me—"

"I didn't save you," he interrupted dryly, removing the cables. "Harley and Brock are not that far."

"Yes, but you saved me from another lecture." She grinned ruefully, and pushed down the hood, locking it. "And I love my sister, I do, but oh, her talks…she can get so serious…and it's bad enough having Mom and Dad lecture, but add in Harley and it's too much."

"Well, glad I could help then." He slammed his own hood and tossed the cables into the rear of the SUV. "And we'll keep this meeting our secret to keep you from getting another scolding."

"Fine. It's a deal. But since you're here, do you want to see the school?"

He glanced past her to the little building with the small, wooden front porch with a short unpainted railing, and an equally plain wooden front door flanked by two tall windows to maximize the light. Five more windows ran the length of the school, the windows trimmed in a dirty white, the siding painted a faded red. "It's not very big."

"No. There's not much to it," she agreed. "It'd be a very quick tour."

He could tell from her expression—so hopeful and excited—that she wanted to show him and it was impossible to tell her no. He didn't know how it'd happened but he'd come to like her quite a bit, and he felt very protective of her. "I'd love to see."

"Come on. We'll leave my car running. Nobody is going to take it."

He glanced around, seeing nothing but moonlight on snowcapped mountains, an empty road in front, with a pasture and a crumbling log cabin on the far side. Somewhere behind the schoolhouse was the river. "Because there is nobody anywhere."

"That's why they're talking about closing the school. Fifteen years ago kids from six or seven families attended this school, and they were big families so there were enough children to make it worthwhile, but today it's just four small families, which is why it's no longer economical."

"So they'd bus the kids into Marietta?"

She nodded, leading the way up the small porch and unlocking the front door. "But bus service up into the mountains is treacherous in winter, which is why they left the school open as long as they have." She turned on the lights and stepped aside to let him enter the school.

Shane closed the door behind him. They were in a little enclosed entry lined with hooks and wooden cubbies on the ground. "This is where the kids keep their lunches, snow boots, and coats," she said, before heading through a wide opening into the main room. "And this is where I teach."

"It's like a freezer in here."

She nodded. "It's cold."

"Where is your heater?"

"We have an old furnace in the back and then I'll plug in

a space heater on really cold days."

"I'd plug in more than one."

"If you do that, you'll blow a fuse. Electrical is old, too. That's why I can only have a mini refrigerator and a low watt microwave."

His gaze swept the tidy rows of desks. There were about twenty desks. "You have twenty students?"

"We had thirteen. That family's gone as of last week, so we're down to twelve."

"What happened to that student?"

"The Hainsleys decided to try a new Christian academy in Livingston."

"Is there a bus to that school?"

"No, the parents are going to drive Jamie each way. They thought it would be better for her. I think they hoped a Christian curriculum would be preferable."

He shot her a narrowed glance. "Why?"

"They don't believe in evolution, or sex education."

"Ah." His brow wrinkled. "Do you teach sex ed?"

"To the older ones, yes."

"And what do the younger ones do while you teach the birds and the bees?"

"Work at their desks."

"Wouldn't they be listening in?"

"I teach the health stuff in a very quiet voice." Her cheeks turned pink.

"How I'd love to be a fly on the wall for that," he answered.

She made a face; cheeks still rosy and blue eyes impossibly bright. "Thank goodness you're not. It takes a lot of work for me to be really calm and matter of fact."

"But as a farm girl, I'm sure you're comfortable with…the mechanics."

She choked on a smothered laugh and then shook her head. "That's terrible, but you're not far off. These are all children of ranchers. They've grown up hunting and fishing and helping out on the property. Sometimes I feel like they know more about the real world than I do."

"I know you've only been here for a little over a month, but do you feel like you've gotten a sense of the importance of this school? Is it an archaic way to teach, or is there a value to keeping the school open…beyond the obvious that it's historically significant?"

"I love that question because I wondered that, too, and while I haven't been here for any of the big events, I've been told that the Christmas play and spring picnic and eighth grade graduation are all huge events, drawing people for miles. Apparently everyone in the valley comes, not just the students' families, but the entire community because this school is the heart of the community, and it keeps everyone connected."

"I would think the local churches serve that purpose."

"But the churches are divided into denominations, and this isn't about a denomination, but the families that live here and call Paradise Valley home. Nearly every student here has a parent who attended this school, and those parents' parents came here, and so it goes, stretching back four and five generations."

He watched her face as she talked. She was pretty and fresh and animated and he could imagine how her students must hang onto her every word.

At least he hung on to every word.

He liked listening to her, and watching her. When she was excited about something her eyes lit up and her expression was bright and light. But then, Jet radiated light. It was a special magic inside of her, the thing that made her irresistible, the thing that warmed him and made him want to pull her close and wrap his arms around her and keep her safe. She deserved to be protected. Cherished. Not that he was the one to do it. God knew he wasn't the relationship sort. He was good at paying for things, whipping out a credit card and picking up expensive dinners and buying pretty trinkets, but connecting...loving? Not his forte.

She was so different from who he'd expected her to be, so much more in every way, and she had the sweet, bubbly side he'd seen while watching her these past few weeks, but she had another side—smart, thoughtful, inquisitive—and he liked talking to her, liked that she wanted to discuss ideas and not just things.

In the past few years, he'd met far too many beautiful women who were more concerned with Instagram and

Snapchat than what was happening in the world, and while he appreciated beauty, he was bored by the shallow, superficiality of a social media driven culture. A year ago he'd sat across from a woman on a flight who'd spent easily—no exaggeration—ten minutes flipping her hair, adjusting her sunglasses on top of her head, taking the sunglasses off, pouting, pursing lips, making duck lips all to get a perfect shot of herself, which she then spent another five to ten minutes doctoring with filters, and her intense self-absorption had fascinated and repelled him at the same time.

How exquisitely, painfully narcissistic...

He'd vowed then to nix dates with Instagram accounts filled with nothing but images of themselves.

When he first left school and started out on his career, the pretty young self-absorbed things hadn't bothered him so much. As a loner, he hadn't wanted a woman for conversation. He was happy to just look at her, and if the physical was satisfying, he was satisfied. But he was almost thirty-five and the shallow and empty left him feeling shallow and empty. Better to be alone, than with someone that left him cold inside.

And he'd been cold, for so long now he'd begun to wonder if the issue wasn't others, but himself. He'd wondered if perhaps he'd been a loner so long that he didn't know how to form real attachments. Perhaps the years of being shuffled around had damaged him completely...

But standing here in this freezing school, he wasn't cold.

If anything, he felt warm, surprisingly warm.

And even more surprising...*happy.*

"I'm definitely coming one day to see you teach," he said. "Not so I can yap, but I want to sit in the back and just watch you and the kids."

"Why?"

"I think it'd be interesting. You're interesting." He smiled at her. "Maybe a little too interesting because I'd rather be with you than working on my book."

"But you're close to the end, right?"

He thought of his desk, and the piles of notes, and the months of research that had ground to a halt as he'd hit one dead end after another. "Not as much as I need," he confessed.

"But you'll get it. You will," she said.

He looked down into her upturned face, her pale brow knitting, her wide, blue eyes narrowing with concern. Her worry made something inside him tighten and ache. He did not want to disappoint her. She believed in him. He couldn't let her down.

"I'm missing key pieces that I need to move forward, and that happens in every book, but not usually at this point—" He broke off, unable to continue, hating to hear himself share his failure yet again, *out loud,* twice in one day. He was never so open, not at all comfortable revealing chinks in his armor.

"And?" she prompted after a moment.

"It's stressful. The book is due in a couple months and I hate feeling as if I am running out of time."

A deep crease formed between her eyebrows. "Is there anything I can do? Any way I can help? Something I can type for you, or research? I'm pretty good with research."

He smiled, touched by the offer, as well as her sincerity. She meant it. She wasn't trying to make points or placate him. "I don't think your family would approve," he reminded her gently. "But thank you. I appreciate your support more than you know."

And then he kissed her, lightly, sweetly, just because she was lightness and sweetness and everything he liked best. "We should go check on your car," he said gruffly, sweeping his thumb across her warm, pink cheek because he didn't want to let her go, but she wasn't his, and couldn't be his and so he forced himself to step away. "Make sure it's still out there, running."

DRIVING HOME, JET thought about the kiss and Shane's book and his worry about the deadline and she wanted to turn her car around and drive back to Paradise Valley and do something for him, do something to help him, even if it was just to make him dinner while he settled back at his desk.

She wasn't a great cook, either, so it'd have to be pasta or maybe a simple broiled steak and baked potato, but he could eat and she could maybe get on the Internet and look up stuff, or go to the library and research...

But he was right that the Sheenan family wouldn't be happy if she helped him in any way, and she'd made Harley a promise just this morning to try to keep her distance from Shane.

She didn't want to keep her distance though.

Today, when he kissed her she wanted to lean in, wanted more of the kiss, more pressure, not less. The kiss had been so fleeting. It had teased her, stirring her senses but leaving her wanting so much more.

When he'd lifted his head, her pulse was jumping and her lips tingled and she couldn't remember when she last felt so alive. And yet it had been just a brief kiss.

Imagine if it had been more…

SHANE RETURNED TO the ranch, feeling better for the break. He'd only been gone thirty or forty minutes total, but the visit to the schoolhouse jarred a memory, and he suddenly needed to have another look at the church program in the Bible on the bookshelf in the Sheenan living room.

During the tour of the school, Jet had said that the school served the entire valley, making it the heart of the valley and a community center.

Tugging off his coat, he tossed it onto the bannister railing before heading across to the living room with its cold hearth and mostly empty bookshelves flanking the mantel. Last night he'd given the Bible a cursory glance but suddenly he was curious about the church bulletin inserted into the

Bible.

Crossing the living room, he retrieved the book with the stiff, black leather binding. Opening the book, he flipped to the bookmarked page, the one he'd seen last night, and looked more closely at the printed bulletin.

July 27-August 4 1996
The New Awakening
Pastor Sawyer Newsome

There it was. Why hadn't he noticed the name and dates last night?

He carried the Bible and church program to the couch and sat down to inspect both.

The New Awakening was a revival, held every year during the summer in that big field behind the one room schoolhouse.

The preacher and his lay people would park their trailers at the far end of the parking lot, and then erect a huge white tent for the worship services. The revival had been in town just a week when the Douglases were murdered, abruptly ending the revival. After that summer, Pastor Newsome never returned.

Early in his research, Shane had spent several long days researching the itinerant, evangelical group which crisscrossed the Pacific Northwest, traveling from Southern Oregon to Eastern Montana each year, preaching salvation by committing to a personal relationship with Jesus Christ through prayer, good work, and self-sacrifice. Newsome had as many critics as supporters. Depending on the perspective, Sawyer Newsome was either heaven-sent, or wildly delusional.

Even the critics, though, couldn't ignore Sawyer Newsome's ability to stir the audience. He drew crowds and created devoted followers with his passionate, charismatic speeches.

The 1996 revival was New Awakening's sixth visit to Paradise Valley. They'd arrived for two weeks of sermons, services, and prayer groups. The tent was just beginning to fill for the Thursday evening service on August first when they heard the first siren, and then the second, and then the third.

And the fourth.

And the fifth.

Ambulances, fire trucks, sheriff patrol cars.

More patrol cars.

And more.

The start of the service was delayed as people tried to decide if they should go see if they were needed. The valley ranchers were a relatively tight-knit group, and while not always friends, they pulled together in emergencies.

The fleet of emergency vehicles was ominous indeed.

Some ranchers left. Others stood ready by their trucks, waiting for word, or the signal, that they were needed. And then a car careened into the lot with news that the entire

Douglas family had been murdered in their own home.

Pastor Newsome tried to turn the evening's service into a prayer vigil but families were unnerved. A family had been senselessly slaughtered and nobody knew who did it. The killer, or killers, was still on the loose. He—they—could be anywhere. People raced home to arm themselves, barricading their families behind locked doors.

Saturday evening when no one showed up for the service, Pastor Newsome took down the tent, packed up the folding chairs, hitched the trailers, and left for Cheyenne.

And that was when people began to talk.

The authorities caught up with Pastor Newsome in Wyoming. Sawyer and his "people" were interrogated, but there was nothing to tie them to the murders. Indeed, Sawyer Newsome was in the middle of leading a group of local ladies in prayer when the murders took place. All of his deacons were on the school grounds, too. It couldn't be them.

But people still wondered, speculating, as Caroline Grace Douglas attended the revival every year without fail, often with one or more of the Douglas children. The younger ones would go to the Bible "camp," and the older ones would join Grace in the tent for the worship service.

But then others dismissed the speculation as dozens of local families participated in the revival each summer. The New Awakening revival had become as much a part of summer as the Fourth of July picnic and the September rodeo. It was unthinkable that Pastor Newsome—a man of

God—could be involved with something that was clearly the work of the devil.

In his research, Shane discovered all the interviews the detectives conducted with those who attended the revival, getting statements, checking facts and leads. The detectives believed they'd spoken with everyone, but how could they be sure?

Now, seated on the couch with the Bible and bulletin, Shane flipped the bulletin over, scanning the scriptures, songs, and prayers before carefully sliding it back into the Bible where he'd found it and flipping through the rest of the Bible. There were more pages underlined, more delicate pencil marks, and then at the front he saw the flash of a name. *Catherine Jeanette Cray.*

He went back to that very first page. The name had been written in an unruly black script at the top of the first page of the book, and he lightly touched her name, written in that ragged, not quite confident calligraphy—Catherine Jeanette Cray. His mother.

This was her Bible.

He felt a hitch in his breath, his chest growing tight.

He was almost thirty-five and he still knew so little about her. He'd spent his life trying to come to terms with the mother who never returned for him, and seeing her girlish handwriting made him feel conflicting emotions. He didn't want to like her, but he loved her. He didn't want to care about her, and yet he still needed her. Or, at the very least, to come to some kind of peace with her.

On the inside of the front cover there was an inscription from an Aunt Olive.

He didn't know of an Aunt Olive. But apparently there was one. His past was like a shadowy cave with dark tunnels in every direction. It was easy to get lost. Easy to become confused. Over the years Shane had begun to fill in some of the missing pieces of his past—the Finley was a maternal great-grandfather, and Cray a maternal grandfather, and Swan the first name that had belonged to the Finely great-grandfather—but there were still so many things that didn't make sense. Why had his grandmother felt the need to give him so many names? Why not just call him Shane Swan? Why add the Finley? Why the subterfuge, if there had indeed been subterfuge? Or had his grandmother simply been misunderstood by all around her?

Questions, and doubts, and a never ending mystery…

Just like the damn book he was writing.

He'd never set out to become a writer, but stories came to him, stories and questions, and Shane could never resist a puzzle, or a mystery.

Which was why he was here, sitting on an old, uncomfortable sofa in the home of a family that should have been by all rights his family, and yet they were strangers. Strangers who hated him.

They were arrogant, too.

The simmering rage boiled up, making his chest hot and

his stomach burn. He didn't like the anger, didn't like the way he felt when his temper stirred, but every time he thought of their attitude and their arrogance.

Their house. *Their* land. *Their* community. *Their* name. *Their* reputation.

The Sheenans acted as if they were lords of a small kingdom. Marietta and Paradise Valley belonged to them. Perhaps they didn't rule with iron fists, but they had tremendous influence. In a matter of weeks they'd turned much of Marietta against him.

He was certain they'd inherited the arrogance and pride from their father, William Sheenan. He'd read plenty about his biological father. His biological father had not been a kind man. He'd certainly had enemies, neighbor rancher Hawksley Carrigan, for one. Shane knew all about the land and water dispute. The two had feuded for over thirty years.

Shane would have liked to have met his father, just once. He would have liked to stand toe to toe with Bill Sheenan and look him in the eye. It would have been easy to do. They were the same height. Six-foot-one.

Shane had seen pictures of him as a young man, and Shane definitely had the Sheenan cheekbones, jaw, and mouth—one of the reasons he wore a beard—but he had his mother's nose, as well as her coloring. All his brothers but Cormac had her coloring. He wished there were photos of her as a young girl. He would have liked to see what she looked like as a child. He'd been surprised when he moved in last spring that there were no photos of her in the house. He'd wondered if they were all in the master bedroom, locked away. The master bedroom was the only room that had a lock. Shane was free to roam the house, but the master bedroom was strictly off limits.

Shane hadn't cared initially. Now, knowing he had just a month left here, he wondered what secrets there were behind the locked door.

Shane stroked the page with his mother's name one last time, and then down the page before flipping it over to a page with a list of events and dates. Important events that needed to be recorded—her confirmation, and then years later, her marriage to William Sheenan on September 1974, and then the birth of each baby.

1975   Brock
1979   Troy & Trey
1981   Cormac
1982
1985   Dillon

He froze. There it was. It was what he'd been looking for all these years—not for the Douglas story, but his. 1982, his birth year. And no, his name hadn't been recorded, but the year he'd been born had been recorded with all the others.

He stared at the blank space next to the date, finding it significant, wondering if anyone else in the family had ever bothered to look at her Bible, and noticed the empty spot next to the year. Perhaps it meant nothing to his brothers. Perhaps they thought it referenced a miscarriage or still birth.

But it meant something to him. It meant that his mother had recognized the birth, and she'd included it in her Bible, in the record of her life, in the history of her family.

In a very small way he mattered. In a very small way he'd existed…even if only for her.

Chapter Seven

J ET USUALLY ATTENDED the nine a.m. church service with Harley and the kids at St. James, but when she woke Sunday morning there was a text from Harley saying that Mack had woken up in the night with a stomach bug and Harley didn't want to risk exposing anyone so they were staying home. Which meant Jet was free.

Jet could have skipped church, but she didn't. She went to the hour-long service and then afterwards walked to Main Street where she joined the line at Java Café for a croissant stuffed with scrambled eggs and cheese, but the line moved with agonizing slowness. Finally she placed her order for the eggs and croissant and a latte with an extra shot, and then searched for a place to sit.

A couple at a table for four said she could join them and then returned to their conversation. Jet didn't want to listen in so she pulled out her phone and pretended to be checking email and Instagram, but it was impossible to ignore the conversation when she realized they were discussing the Douglas family and the murders on the ranch.

"Only three of the six Douglas kids survived, all the older

ones," the woman said to her boyfriend. "The oldest son was gone, driving someone to a party, so that's why those two survived, but the rest were shot."

"They all died?" the man asked.

"Everyone but Quinn. You know Quinn Douglas. He's that outfielder that was just signed by Seattle."

"His family was killed?"

"And he was shot like four or five times. He was supposed to die. The fact that he didn't was a miracle."

"But everyone else died?"

"Yes."

"Why was he left alive?"

"I don't know...maybe they thought he was dead?"

Jet couldn't move. Her ears felt like they were burning while the rest of her was icy cold. She didn't want to sit here and listen to them discuss the murders, feeling a fierce protectiveness towards McKenna, understanding for the first time what it felt like hearing absolute strangers discuss a family she knew as if they were the Kardashians.

This was why the Sheenans were angry about the book. This was why they didn't want the book to happen, and yet, listening to the details, she found herself drawn into the conversation, and she knew it wasn't because of McKenna but Shane. "Excuse me," she said, interrupting the couple's discussion. "I've just recently moved to the area. Do you live here?"

"I used to," the girl answered, tearing a chunk from her

bagel. "I'm going to grad school in Missoula but Michael and I thought it'd be fun to head this way for a weekend ski trip and a visit to Marietta."

"Did you live here at the time of the Douglas ranch tragedy?" Jet asked.

The girl nodded. "I was only five but I remember hearing my parents talk about it late at night in their bedroom. My dad told my mom to keep a gun on her always and not to be afraid to use it. He said with a murderer on the loose it was better not to take chances."

Jet was fascinated. "What did your mother say?"

"She cried. She was scared. She didn't want Dad to leave her for work, but he had to. He was one of the foremen on the Circle C Ranch and work had to be done."

"The Circle C Ranch?"

"The Carrigans' ranch in Paradise Valley. We lived on the ranch, so we were right there where it all happened."

Jet pushed her half-eaten croissant away. "So you were neighbors?"

She nodded again. "Just up the road from the Douglases. That's what made it so scary. The killer could be any one of the people living in the area, or hiding in the hills, or in one of the old homesteads, or maybe even in one of the abandoned mines..." Her voice drifted away. "Mom couldn't handle it. Eventually we moved to town, and then later, they divorced." She was silent for a beat and then added, "My mom used to say that whoever did it killed two families...the

Douglas' and ours."

The girl's boyfriend reached over and covered her hand with his. Jet looked at their linked fingers and then blurted, "You know that a book is being written about the tragedy." She didn't know why she said that, but she was curious about the girl's response.

"Good," the girl answered firmly. "Maybe they'll finally catch that a-hole—or a-holes. Whoever did it should be punished."

"Do you think most people feel that way?"

"That the murderer should be punished?"

"About the book being written."

"I think people will be okay with the book if it solves the crime. Otherwise…what's the point?"

The girl's boyfriend began stacking their plates and Jet knew they were about to leave but she had to ask one last question.

"Who did your mom think did it? Did she ever say?"

The girl shrugged. "She didn't know. That's why she started to hate the ranch. It made her feel crazy."

The boyfriend stood and the girl stood. Jet did, too. "So no theories?"

"Lots of people said it might have been one of those seasonal ranch hands, or even someone who'd once worked for Mr. Douglas, but my mom thought it wasn't about Mr. Douglas, but Mrs. Douglas."

"Why Mrs. Douglas?"

"She was really beautiful. Many people say she was the most beautiful girl to ever come out of Crawford County. She was Miss Montana, did you know that?"

Jet shook her head.

"I don't know exactly what happened," the girl added, "but she gave up her crown after just a few months. She didn't like being in the spotlight—I think she had some weird fans or maybe just one really obsessive fan—but it freaked her out and she left midyear, which was a big scandal in and of itself, and then got really religious afterwards, always attending church and Bible studies and revivals."

"So whoever committed the crimes could have been obsessed with Mrs. Douglas?"

"That's what my mom says. Maybe even some sicko involved with that weird church."

"Weird church?"

"Traveling preacher. Thought he was the new Messiah or something. Now that is an interesting story."

The boyfriend had exited onto the street and the girl hurried to catch up. Jet accompanied her out. "Where is your mom now?"

"She lives in Polson. Runs a shoe store with my stepdad."

"Thank you so much." Jet extended her hand. "By the way, I'm Jet Diekerhof. I'm teaching at the one room schoolhouse in Paradise Valley. You've been really helpful."

"Laura," the girl replied, shaking her hand. "Glad I could

help." And then Laura and her boyfriend, Michael, were walking away.

Jet watched them a moment, thinking of everything just discussed, and then she thought of Shane and his book and all the rumors and scandal and how important it was that the book that was being written was correct, that he laid to rest the gossip and rumors and focused on the truth.

She shouldn't get involved. She shouldn't. But maybe it was too late for that. Jet reached into her purse for her phone and shot Shane a text. *I learned some interesting things today about Douglas ranch. Interested?*

He answered almost right away. *Yes.* Then added in a new text. *Heading off to ski right now, but should be home around two. Should I call then?*

Sure. Or I could drop by and tell you, she answered.

He didn't hesitate. *Drop by.*

JET HAD A little over two hours to kill before she drove out to Shane's. She knew approximately where the Sheenan ranch was as Harley had taken her on a tour of Marietta and Paradise Valley when Jet had first arrived, but needed to double check the actual road as the Sheenan ranch was an earlier exit than her schoolhouse, but then set deep in the valley, up in the foothills of the Absarokas, facing the Gallatin Mountain Range.

Jet pulled up the map app on her phone and noted the exit she'd take off Highway 89 and then the winding road that looped the valley, connecting back with the highway just north of Pray. It'd take her twenty-five minutes or so to get to the Sheenan's, leaving her an hour and a half to either get some work done, or watch TV, or maybe do a little research of her own into the Douglas ranch murders. She didn't really know the story and if she was going to try to help Shane then she needed to know what really happened, which meant gathering the facts.

Checking her watch, Jet realized the library would now be open so she walked quickly down Main Street, towards the courthouse in Crawford Park before cutting through the parking lot on Court Street for the library.

The library's parking lot only had a few cars in it, which wasn't unusual for a Sunday. Jet climbed the front steps, the handsome building one of the first built in turn-of-the-century Marietta in the heyday of the copper mining boom, hoping Taylor Sheenan, Marietta's new head librarian, would not be working today.

Jet had always liked Taylor but she was still annoyed Taylor had told the others that she'd spotted Jet talking to Shane at Java Café last week. Just like it was none of Cormac's business that she'd had dinner with Shane Friday night.

Harley had put the squeeze on Jet to stay away from Shane but Jet wasn't sure she could.

Thank goodness there was no one Jet recognized at the library's front desk so she asked the librarian on duty, an older woman with a welcoming smile, if they saved the local newspapers, and if so, how far back did they go.

The librarian answered they had newspapers dating back almost one hundred years, although most of those early ones were fragile and rarely handled.

"What about papers from the 1990's, would any of those be available?"

"I would think so. What are you looking for?"

Jet drew a quick breath. "Papers that would be covering the Douglas ranch murders."

The librarian hesitated a moment before calmly answering, "That would be 1996. August. The murders took place on the first."

Jet met her gaze. "Could I have the papers for that first week?"

"Give me a few minutes and I'll bring them out to you. Where will you be sitting?"

Jet nodded to one of the empty tables not far from the magazine racks. "Right there."

The woman returned a few minutes later with the papers. "Are you a journalist, too?" she asked, placing the papers on the table in front of Jet.

Interesting. Shane must have been here researching. "No. I'm a teacher."

"History?"

"It's one of the subjects I teach. I'm at the Paradise Valley one room schoolhouse, just south of Emigrant Gulch."

"Didn't they hire a new teacher just a year or two ago?"

"Yes, Missy Sharp, but she's on maternity leave and I'm filling in for the rest of the school year." Jet held out her hand. "By the way, I'm Jet Diekerhof."

"I'm Louise Jenkins." Louise glanced towards the front desk, making sure no one was waiting for her. No one was. It was still late morning and the library was practically empty. "Your last name—Diekerhof—sounds awfully familiar, but I'm not able to place it."

"You might know my sister, Harley. She's now married to Brock Sheenan—"

"I do. Harley, yes. She's a lovely woman. She used to always bring the twins in once a week and I'd help them find books. I used to be the children's head librarian but I retired last year and now just fill in when I'm needed." Louise beamed at Jet. "So pleased to meet you. This is a wonderful surprise. I take it Harley helped get you the job?"

"She did. I'm grateful."

"And now you want to know about the tragedy on the Douglas ranch."

Jet squirmed. "I don't want to know, but there's so much talk about it right now, and it's a sensitive subject with the Sheenans so they never say much."

"Is there a lot of talk?"

"I think so. Or maybe I'm just hearing about it because the Sheenans are upset about Sean Finley's book." Jet's brow furrowed. "I take it he's been here and talked to you about it."

"Yes. Mr. Finely—" Louise broke off as a mother and her three young children approached the front desk, arms full of books. "Let me go help them. Have a look at these and I'll check back on you when I have a moment."

Jet didn't even have to unfold the first paper to read the headlines. It covered the top quarter of the page, the font huge and black and shocking.

Massacre on the Douglas Ranch. 5 Dead.

Jet exhaled slowly, feeling her heart already pound. She wasn't one who liked horror films. She didn't enjoy being scared. And this was real.

Spreading the paper out, Jet began to read.

Just skimming the story chilled her. She felt sick by the time she was finished with the first article. Jet glanced up at the date on the paper. Friday, August second.

The first days of the last month of summer before school started.

The older boys, Rory and Quinn, had only been home an hour or so from their high school football practice, the infamous hell week at Marietta High.

Rory, sixteen, had been asked to drive thirteen year old McKenna to a friend's for a sleepover.

Quinn had headed into the barn to do chores. And then it had happened. The violent assault—

"Pretty horrific, isn't it?"

Jet jumped at the sound of Louise's voice. She nodded. "I feel sick," she whispered, unable to get the words out of her head, unable to imagine the horror Rory found on returning to the ranch after dropping McKenna in town. He had to race to the neighbor's since, at the time, there was no cell coverage and the phone's landline had been cut.

"By far the darkest point in Marietta's history," Louise said.

"You lived here then?"

"I've lived here all my life."

"You remember it all?"

"I do."

Taylor lifted the next paper and then the one after, and the front page of each was filled with more gruesome head-lines. ***Bloodbath on Local Ranch. Baby Slain in Crib. Young Victim Still Clinging to Life.***

"And these headlines?" Jet said. "All true?"

Louise nodded. "The nine-year-old tried to save his baby sister."

Jet swallowed hard, blinking back tears. "Quinn, the boy that was hurt, but survived?"

"He was in ICU for weeks. He wasn't supposed to make it. He crawled all the way from the barn to the driveway. That's where Rory found him. He was trying to get help. Thank God for Rob MacCreadie and Bill Sheenan. They rushed to the scene, saved that boy. Both of them gave blood later. The whole town did. People lined up to donate blood. Everyone wanted to do something for those kids."

"Was Quinn able to identify the attackers?"

"No. He was gunned down in the barn while taking care of horses."

"He was just a teenager."

"Almost sixteen. Just about to start his sophomore year of high school."

"How is he now? Okay?"

"He's fine. He recovered and went on to become a major league baseball player. He just signed a one-year contract with the Seattle Mariners and many expect this to be his last year."

So that's the baseball player Laura and Michael were discussing at Java Café. "Did he have a good career?"

"Excellent. But he wouldn't have survived those early days if Rory and McKenna hadn't stayed by his side, day and night. The hospital even put another bed in Quinn's room to be sure someone could always be there with him."

"Where is Rory now?"

"Still around, at least when he's not competing on the IBR."

"IBR?"

"International Bull Riders circuit." Louise grimaced. "Talk about a rough sport. Don't understand why anyone would want to do that."

"There's got to be money, otherwise, why do it?" Jet agreed, thinking about everything she'd read and heard. "So what happened to the kids afterwards?"

"Their mother's sister, Karen, took them in for a bit. She used to live north of Livingston in a little town called Clyde Park, but she sold her house and bought something close to the high school. McKenna and Quinn lived with her after Quinn was released from the hospital."

"And Rory?"

"He wanted to live with friends in Marietta. He was a senior and a star wide receiver and everyone wanted Rory to have a normal senior year...or as normal as it could be, considering. The town rallied around those kids. No one wanted to see them get sent to foster care, not after what they'd been through, and even though they are no longer teenagers, those three still mean a lot to Marietta."

"So who did it?"

Louise shook her head. "No one knows."

"No one has any suspicion? No person of interest that wasn't charged for whatever reason?"

"There has been so much speculation that I hate to weigh in. It doesn't help."

"I met someone today whose father was a ranch foreman for the Circle C and she mentioned a traveling church that came to Paradise Valley every summer. Do you know anything about that?"

Louise's expression firmed. "Pastor Newsome. Went once to hear him preach but didn't like his message, or some of the people he traveled with, and never went back."

"Could he have been involved?"

"He was leading a Bible study at the time so it wasn't him, but he had some odd followers. They were a little too zealous. Wasn't for me, and OC—my husband—agreed."

"How were his followers odd?"

"Now you sound like Mr. Finley. He asked me that, too, when he interviewed me."

"People are upset about the book he's writing. Does his book bother you, too?"

She hesitated. "I know Mr. Finley's work and the quality of his writing and research, so in theory, I don't have an issue. But as someone who has watched over those Douglas kids, and fretted over their well-being, it's difficult."

"So you wouldn't try to stop it."

"I don't believe in censorship. I'm a librarian." She smiled, and then her smile faded. "But it's not an easy subject. I grew up with Grace Gordon—that was Grace Douglas' maiden name—and she was a very dear friend. What happened to her, and her family, in that home still haunts me to this day. I'll never forget visiting with Catherine Sheenan not long after the murders, and Catherine said, *'That could have been me.'* And Catherine's words stuck with me, because I think every woman in this community felt that way."

JET WAS USUALLY quite comfortable driving Highway 89. After six weeks of commuting to Emigrant Gulch for the teaching job, she knew the road well. It was just one lane in each direction and traveling south, the Yellowstone River was on her left, a dark glimmer against the patchy snow on the riverbanks.

The sun was trying hard to shine through the heavy clouds that gathered over the Absarokas, and Jet appreciated the effort as she battled a fit of nerves.

Harley would not be happy if she found out about Jet visiting Shane on the Sheenan ranch.

But then, no one in the Sheenan family would be happy.

Jet had never thought of herself as a rebel. Yes, she'd always had a mind of her own, as well as a strong sense of self, but she'd never broken "rules," she hadn't ever caused trouble. Even as a teenager she hadn't been contrary, too intent on excelling in school, too determined to be a success. So Jet didn't know why she felt so compelled to see Shane. She didn't like conflict. She didn't want to stir things up. And yet here she was, heading straight into potential heartache.

Uncomfortable with the direction of her thoughts, and the butterflies in her middle, she forced her attention to the narrow road taking her deeper into the rolling hills. The smaller houses and acre properties lining the river gave way to larger spreads. Rustic signs and cattle guards marked the entrance to different properties. One of them was the entrance to the MacCreadie ranch. Another was the entrance to the Douglas'. And then the Sheenan's, the big iron "S" dangling from a wooden beam the only indication she'd reached the entrance to their property. She knew from hearing the Sheenans talk the ranch had been in the family for almost a hundred years. The first Sheenan had arrived in Montana in the 1890s but didn't have the money to buy the current property until the 1920s. It was a big property, too, and the only other family spread that rivaled the size of the Sheenan ranch was the Carrigan's, owners of the Circle C, the ranch east of the Sheenan place.

Jet followed the dusty dirt road a quarter of a mile until it dead-ended in front of a two-story, log cabin ranch house. A relatively modern tractor was parked just in front of a huge weathered barn. Corrals flanked both sides of the barn.

The house wasn't particularly inspiring. Constructed of hand-hewn logs, the house looked solid but lacked what a real estate agent would call curb appeal. The front porch was small and narrow, with an equally small overhang to protect one from rain or snow, but the smallness of the porch and the steepness of the brown roof all looked practical rather than charming. Even the trim on the windows and front door were the same shade of brown as the roof. There were no homey touches, but also, no clutter.

Shane opened the front door before she'd even had a chance to knock.

"Hi there," she said, smiling, thinking he looked ridiculously handsome in his soft, faded Levis and cherry-red Henley shirt. He'd pushed the long sleeves up on his forearms, revealing the intricate ink on one arm. She'd love to see the tattoos without his shirt, curious as to how much of his body they covered. Was it just the arm, or did they extend over his shoulder, too? She didn't think he had tattoos on his chest. At least, the round neckline of the shirt didn't reveal any, just smooth taut skin and the top of his muscular chest. He was built. Muscles everywhere.

She swallowed hard. "I'm not too early am I?"

"Not at all. Welcome," he answered, holding the door wider so she could enter the house.

She felt nervous all over again as he closed the door behind her. "Where did you go skiing?" she asked, trying to sound calm and normal when her pulse was pounding and her confidence was dipping. "Bridger Bowl?"

"I went skate skiing. Over by Miracle Lake."

She was impressed. She'd tried to skate ski once and it was hard. "Did you come home tired?"

"The good kind of tired. Definitely more mellow."

"So you're making good progress on your book."

"No, making very little progress but it was that or lose my mind, and I don't feel like losing my mind."

"Good call." Jet began unsnapping her coat. "Isn't Miracle Lake where all the kids go skating?"

"You haven't been there yet?"

"I don't skate."

"At all?" he asked, taking her coat from her and heading down the long hall.

She followed him. "I can wobble around a little bit.

Maybe even wobble backwards, but it's not pretty. Do you skate?"

"I learned to play hockey at one of the boys' homes. The more aggressive I could appear on the ice, the less aggressive I needed to be off the ice." He hung her coat on a hook near the kitchen. "Hungry? Thirsty?"

"I'd love a cup of tea."

"I'm good at that."

In the kitchen, with the yellow pine cabinets and Formica counters, he moved efficiently from stove to sink, filling the copper kettle, and then back to the stove, placing the dented kettle on a gas burner.

As he busied himself at the stove, she found herself checking him out again. He seemed made for old, faded jeans and soft thermal shirts. She liked the way the knit fabric skimmed his broad chest but wrapped his hard biceps, highlighting the thick muscle. She liked the fit of the Levis and how his dark hair was loose. He'd done something to his beard, too. It was shorter and lighter, as if he'd come close to shaving it all off. She liked him with a beard, but she thought he looked even more handsome with a cleaner jaw. "Looks like you got a little crazy with your razor," she teased.

He glanced at her over his shoulder, expression rueful. "Wasn't intentional. I was trimming the beard and not paying attention. You can't leave one side of your face furrier than the other."

"When did you do that?"

"Just after I got back from skiing. I showered, thought I ought to polish up a bit for you, and then—oops." He lined up two mugs and pulled out a number of boxes of tea. "Which one appeals? English breakfast, peppermint, orange spice, and Earl Grey."

"English breakfast if I can add a splash of milk and sugar."

"You can." He turned around to face her as the water heated. "So does Harley know you're here?"

"No."

"Are you sure this is wise?"

"Probably as long as we don't get married and have babies."

One black eyebrow lifted. "I suppose that rules out me taking you to bed."

One second they'd been bantering and the next the kitchen felt taut and explosive. She felt her cheeks grow hot and her insides do a somersault.

"Probably wise to avoid bedrooms," she agreed, voice husky.

His dark eyes warmed, the expression intent and very male. "Any place else we should avoid?"

Her heart thudded hard and yet her pulse felt like warm honey in her veins, thick, sweet, seductive. "Places with couches and sofas."

"Bad, too, huh?"

"Yeah."

His gaze locked with hers and held. "What about rugs in front of fireplaces?"

"No. Hardwood floors…stone floors…no blazing fires."

"No fires, either?"

She could picture him stretched out over her, kissing her, his hands in her hair, his lips finding every little sensitive spot on her neck…

"Cold hearths are preferable." She choked, her skin prickling, body now hot all over. She'd peel off her sweater if she could but she didn't have anything but a bra underneath. "Cold is good. Hard and uncomfortable even better."

His mouth curved in the most sinful, wicked grin she'd ever seen in her life. "As I'm concerned for your well-being, I would recommend hard is always better, but we can't have uncomfortable. I promise you'd never be uncomfortable."

Jet exhaled in a soft dizzying rush. He was going straight to her head, seducing her with words, and her body loved it. *Traitorous body.*

Thank God the kettle came to a boil and whistled. "You play dirty."

"*I* do?"

"Yes, you."

"You're the one who sent a text that said *I could call, or drop by.*"

"Drop by doesn't mean sex."

"No, but drop by means I could see you, in person, which for men, is far preferable to phone conversations."

"This is about the Douglas ranch investigation."

He gave her a pointed look before grabbing a hot pad to lift the kettle from the stove and fill the mugs. "Right."

"I'm serious."

Steam swirled from the kettle and mugs. "So am I. I've been told to keep my distance from you or someone is going to cause me bodily harm." He set the kettle down and gave her another pointed glance. "But here you are."

She smiled. She couldn't help it. It was his inflection and the glint in his dark eyes and the easy way he moved about the kitchen, so very comfortable. He'd obviously been a bachelor a long time. "Do you mind so terribly much that I am here?"

"No. I wanted to see you. I like you. And apparently I like a good fight."

Jet choked on smothered laughter. "Nobody is going to put a fist in your face."

"Because Harley and Cormac and the rest of that beast of a family have agreed that we can be friends?" he asked dryly, handing her a cup. "Be careful. It's hot. I don't want you to get burned."

She appreciated the concern. She didn't want to get burned, either. Not by the scalding hot mug, or by his gorgeous fascinating self.

He could hurt her. He'd break her heart if she let him. She couldn't let him. She couldn't drop her guard. Not with him, or anyone. It was too soon after Ben. She wasn't strong enough yet, wasn't ready to love, or trust...

Especially herself.

He reached out suddenly and brushed a tendril from her brow. The long strand tangled on a lash and as he freed the strand his fingertips brushed her cheek.

She inhaled hard, pulse jumping. His touch was electric and everything inside her zinged.

"You okay?" he asked quietly, his voice pitched low, his tone serious.

Her heart drummed even faster. She couldn't look away from his eyes, the irises so dark she felt lost in them. Yesterday when they'd talked, she'd been able to see the boy in him, and yet this afternoon he was all man. A tough, physical, sexual man and she didn't know what to do with him...

Or how to feel about him...

But she knew why she was here. In person. She hadn't wanted to talk on the phone. She'd wanted to be here for this...this hot, crackling, sizzling energy. His hot, crackling, sizzling energy. She must be mad but everything about him intrigued her. He was like the story she just couldn't put down. Beautiful. Unpredictable. And oh, so very compelling.

But did she really need to have her heart broken again? Because he would break it. He was a take no prisoners kind of guy. What she should do was go, before she developed more feelings, before she lost her head altogether.

"So I heard something interesting today," she said huskily, holding her cup in front of her as if it was a shield and able to protect her in battle. "I thought it might prove useful to you somehow."

"I'd love to hear," he said, as if nothing had just happened between them. As if his touch had been nothing…

Maybe it was nothing…

That thought hurt more than it should.

She gulped a breath and dove into her story, desperate to find her footing. "I went to Java Café this morning for breakfast and ended up sharing a table with a couple. They were close to my age and the girl was telling her boyfriend about the Douglas ranch murders. I couldn't help listening. It was impossible not to hear." She paused and took a breath, telling herself to slow down. He wasn't going anywhere. He was listening. Everything was fine.

"What made it interesting," she continued, "is that the girl, Laura, lived on the Carrigan ranch at the time of the murders. Her dad was one of the foremen for the Circle C and even though she was just five, Laura remembered how awful it was then, living in the valley, and how scared everyone was. With the murders unsolved, her mom wanted to leave Paradise Valley. She didn't feel safe so far out, and so they ended up moving to town, and then later her parents divorced."

"Did she say why her parents divorced?"

"Her mom blamed the murders. Laura said something like whoever committed the crime killed two families that day, not one."

"Interesting."

"I asked her if she had any theories on who did it," Jet added.

Shane's eyebrows lifted.

Jet saw his expression and grimaced. "I like knowing things."

He seemed to be struggling to check a smile. "So what did you learn?"

"Laura's mom had two theories about the person who did it. It was either a ranch hand who had a beef with Mr. Douglas over something, or it was someone who had a thing for Mrs. Douglas. Apparently Mrs. Douglas was really beautiful and Laura's mom thought that maybe someone had become obsessed with her and kind of went nuts."

"Mmm. Only I don't think it was a ranch hand."

"Could it have been someone with that revival? The one that visited Paradise Valley in the summer?"

"How did you hear about that?"

"Laura mentioned it and then I asked Louise Jenkins—"

"Louise Jenkins?"

"The librarian. In Marietta."

"When did you talk to her?"

"Today. I went to do some research. They have copies of all the original newspapers."

"I've interviewed her at length."

"She told me."

His lips curved. "You could be a detective."

She smiled crookedly. "I could, couldn't I?"

He was still smiling but he was looking past her, out the window over the kitchen sink, his attention on something else now. Silence followed and Jet could see he was deep in thought. She waited to hear what he'd say, wondering if her information helped him at all.

"I'd love to talk to Laura's mother," he said at last. "Sounds like she has very vivid memories and wouldn't be opposed to telling me what she remembers." His brow creased a little as he turned to look at her again. "She's here in town?"

"No. She's in Polson. I'm not sure where that is, though."

"It's on the south end of Flathead Lake."

"Isn't that where you lived with your grandmother?"

"Yes. And my mom's cabin in Cherry Lake is just north of Polson. Maybe fifteen minutes from the town."

"Is it someplace you'd fly from here or would you drive?"

"I'd drive. It's not that far. Four or five hours, depending on the weather."

"You should go."

"I'm thinking about it." He sipped his hot tea. Steam still rose from the cup. She could see that he was thinking hard on something and then he looked at her intently, dark eyes studying her over the rim of his mug. "Feel like a road trip? Want to go?"

"Go?"

He shrugged. "Why not? It's a beautiful drive. You'd have the chance to see more of Montana." He must have noticed her tell-tale blush. "We'll have separate rooms. I respect the whole avoid the bed-couch-sheepskin-rug-in-front-of-the-fire thing."

Her lips twitched and she had to bite the inside of her cheek to keep from smiling too widely. He was impossible. And apparently she liked that. "There is no way I could hide that from Harley."

"Wouldn't want you to."

"She'd freak."

"She would."

"So it's really a moot point."

"If you're trying to keep peace in the family."

"You don't think I should."

"Not saying that at all. I can't advise you on this one. I have never grown up having to please a big family."

Or any family, she added silently.

"I don't want you in the middle," he said after a half-beat. "I do mean that. So forget I asked. We're going to pretend there was no invitation. You know nothing about my trip to Flathead Lake."

Jet clutched her mug, smashing the disappointment, smashing the wave of hot anger and resentment she felt each time she bumped up against Harley's rules.

Harley hadn't laid down any rules since Jet was a very young girl and Harley would be left in charge of the younger ones, and so Jet was finding it almost impossible to tolerate being issued with rules and edicts now, in part because she'd been on her own several years now, and in part because she just didn't agree with Harley's point of view in the first place.

"You're still going to go, though?" Jet asked, hoping she didn't sound as woebegone as she felt.

"I need to. There are things I want to ask, and these things are always better in person."

"Do people open up more in person than on the phone?"

He hesitated. "With me, yes. Some journalists and researchers prefer emails and phone calls. It allows them to get back to their keyboard faster."

"How do you use interview?"

"Old school. Notepad, pen, and tape recorder."

And now he was sounding like Sean Finley and not Shane Swan and Jet found herself really, *really* wanting to go to Polson, Montana, which sounded like the most fascinating place on earth at that moment in time. "And it's a pretty drive?"

"Incredible drive and incredible scenery when you get there."

"You're torturing me now."

"No, if I wanted to do that, I'd drag you to a couch and kiss you until you—" He broke off, listening to something. His brow furrowed.

Then Jet heard it. A truck hurtling up the driveway.

"Sounds like we have company," Shane said.

Jet went to the kitchen sink and looked out the window and spotted the big, red truck parking in front of the house right next to Jet's car, which was actually Harley's car.

"It's Trey," she said huskily.

Shane took a sip of his tea. "This could be interesting."

But Jet was panicked. "That's an understatement."

Shane leaned against the kitchen counter and took another sip of tea. "Don't worry. I'm—" He was cut off by the sound of a fist hammering on the front door, followed by another hard series of thuds, one, two, three.

Jet set down her tea with a thunk. "That doesn't sound good."

Shane shrugged. "Do you want to head out the back and escape while you can?"

"I'm not in danger, Shane. And hopefully, neither are you." But her voice wobbled as she said it and she hoped she sounded more confident than she felt.

She must not have been very convincing because Shane just laughed.

SHANE WAS AWARE of Jet on his heels as he headed for the front door. He would have preferred for Jet to stay in the kitchen, but she was here, and he was determined to keep things calm, and controlled, for her sake if nothing else.

But opening the front door, Trey's anger was immediately palpable. "I want to see," Trey said roughly. "Show me."

"Show you what?" Shane asked coolly, not at all surprised to see Trey here, just surprised it had taken Trey this long to make an appearance. Cormac and Troy had been in Shane's face for awhile. Had they only recently told Trey about Shane's book?

Trey pushed past Shane, and his narrowed gaze fell on Jet. His jaw hardened. "I don't know what you're doing here," he said to Jet, his deep voice a rumble. "And maybe you think you're somehow helping—"

"We're friends," she said. Her voice was soft, faint, and yet she stood tall, chin lifted as if letting him know she wouldn't be cowed.

Trey seemed to struggle to hold back the first words he wanted to say. Instead, he quirked a brow. "Odd choice for a friend." And then he focused on Shane. "You can either walk me to the dining room, or I'll take myself there. But I want to see it. The bulletin boards. The newspaper clippings. The book. All of it."

Shane turned around and led the way. There was no point in delaying the inevitable. He stepped aside once in the dining room so Trey could see.

Trey entered behind him and then froze.

Shane watched Trey—a man that was apparently his full biological brother—as Trey's gaze swept the room.

Trey looked at everything, taking in the transformation from dining room to office. The antique sideboard had become a printing station. A laptop with stacks of folders was adjacent at the end of the table. The rest of the table was covered with piles of books, notes, reams of printed pages, while the walls behind were lined with bulletin boards with shocking headlines.

Local Family Slain in Home Invasion. Slaughter of Innocents. Tragedy in Marietta. Montana Manhunt.

Trey said nothing for a long time. He just stood there, reading the headlines again and again, arms loose at his sides, and yet his hands were clenched. He was not as calm and collected as he appeared.

"So it's true," he said finally.

Shane didn't answer, certain there was more to come.

Trey turned around and faced him. "You're using *my* family home to profit from *my* wife's tragedy?"

"The house was for lease. I needed a place to work. That's why I'm here."

"And you couldn't have found another house in Paradise Valley?"

"Maybe, but this was the closest to the crime."

"And why was that so important?"

"I don't just sit and write. I explore myself. I've walked the Douglas property, and up and down the easement road a dozen times now."

"I bet you would have broken into Douglas house if it was still standing."

"Probably."

Trey shook his head, disgusted. "How much are you getting paid to do this?"

"That's not why I do it."

"And you're going to tell me you're not making a lot of money from this book? Because I heard your last book was on the *New York Times* bestseller list for over a year. *A year.* Now I don't know a lot about publishing, but I'd suspect that being on a list like that for *a year* means you sold a lot of copies, and you earn a hefty percentage from each copy sold."

"I wouldn't say a hefty percentage," Shane answered.

"But you make good money."

"I've been successful, yes."

"And this book, the one you're writing, when do you turn it in?"

"Soon."

"How soon?"

"April."

"Don't. Don't finish it. Don't do it. Don't put McKenna's family on the *New York Times* for a year. Because I'm sure you've discovered all the things that our local law enforcement managed to keep from the media and there is no need to sensationalize what happened that afternoon eighteen years later. I love this ranch, but I don't live here because my wife still has nightmares about her dad being tortured, and her mom being assaulted, and it didn't happen here, but close to here, and we all lost so much that day.

Every one of us." Trey's hands flexed and balled. His chest rose and fell with deep breath. "I'm sure you uncovered all the juicy tidbits, and I'm sure you'd like to write a whole chapter on a good woman being raped in front of her children and dying husband—"

"There's not a chapter on it. I'm not trying to sensationalize anything," Shane interrupted harshly. "I'm telling what happened, and talking about the bungled investigation after, and focusing on who that person might have been, and why that person was never held accountable. That person should have been held accountable because a good woman was tortured—"

"But doing that, you open deep, deep wounds." Trey's voice was hoarse. "And there will be fresh media attention all over again. We don't need cameras in our faces. We don't need reporters accosting McKenna, waiting on the doorstep, calling her at work, asking horrific questions over and over just to get a juicy sound bite. Our boy TJ is a first-grader. He doesn't know anything about this. And he shouldn't, not until he's older. Let him have his innocence. Let him be a child a little longer. Don't finish your book. Don't make my family your meal ticket—"

"You're *not* a meal ticket."

"You can write other books but this is ours...our horror, our pain...it shouldn't become a public circus, not again."

"I have a contract. The book is already in production—"

"They can't publish something if you don't turn it in."

"I do not not turn things in. It would kill my career if I failed to deliver."

"You're not allowed to change your mind?"

"Not after I've been paid."

"Give the money back."

"It's not that simple."

"What if you got sick? What if you couldn't finish it?"

"That won't happen."

"What if you were no longer able to write?"

"Is that a threat?"

"I am not prepared to tell my six-year-old that his mother's family was slain in a bloody rampage. I am not."

"I'm not unsympathetic—"

"Bastard." The oath was followed by Trey's right fist, colliding with Shane's jaw.

Pissed off, as much by the blow as by the curse, Shane responded with a swift, hard undercut that would have sent anyone else flying, but Trey merely rocked back a step before coming back for more.

Jet was making a racket in the background, yelling at them to stop, but neither of them listened, too busy throwing punches, quick, controlled blows, much like boxers in a ring. Trey was a good fighter, Shane would give him that, but Shane had skills, too.

He would have never survived if he hadn't learned to protect himself—and others. But right now this wasn't about protecting himself. Right now this was about establishing himself. Introducing who he really was.

Not some hipster writer from Manhattan, but a Sheenan.

His "brothers" might be tough, but he was just as strong, just as committed. He didn't just hold his own, he could go the distance.

"What the hell do you want?" Trey growled, slamming his fist into Shane's gut.

Shane coughed, the wind temporarily knocked out of him, but he came back with a swift fist to Trey's face. Blood spurted from Trey's nose.

"What are you asking?" Shane asked, tasting blood from his split lip.

"Tell me what you're getting for this book and I'll pay you the same not to publish it."

"You couldn't afford it."

"You've no idea what I can afford. You've no idea about my finances." Trey landed a blow on the side of Shane's head. "Asshole."

That one made Shane see stars. He blinked and quickly wiped the blood from his lip. "It's seven figures plus. And then there's the film deal. And foreign rights. Audio." He threw a punch at Trey's jaw, which Trey blocked this time.

"Total it up. I'll draft a contract. We'll make the deal."

"But there's no deal." Shane was able to land a low one, in Trey's belly. "My book and my business—"

"About my *wife*." Trey slammed his fist into Shane's cheekbone, and then a quick second into his nose.

Again Shane saw stars. He was beginning to tire but there was no way he'd give up. Not now. Not ever. "It's not about her," Shane gritted, feeling blood on his upper lip now. His nose must be bleeding too, now. "It's about a crime no one solved, and it should be solved." He danced back, dodging Trey's fist. "Unless there's a very good reason why it shouldn't…can you think of one?"

"What kind of question is that?"

"Maybe a Sheenan was involved. Maybe one of your brothers—"

Trey connected this time, making Shane stumble backwards. He struggled to stay on his feet. "Don't ever say that again." Trey gave Shane a hard shove.

Shane pushed him right back. "If you care so much about your wife, find out who killed her family! Don't you think she deserves that? Doesn't she deserve closure? Or is she supposed to go through her whole life wondering what the hell happened to her family? What the hell happened to her life?"

It wasn't until Shane had his hand wrapped around Trey's throat that he realized Trey was no longer fighting back.

Trey was just standing there, staring into Shane's eyes. "I don't want her hurt anymore," he said quietly, roughly. "She's been through enough."

Shane dropped his hand but he didn't step away. He stayed where he was…which was right in Trey's face. "It's not to hurt her. It's to answer questions no one has been able to answer."

"And can you? Or are you just stirring things up for a million-dollar contract? Because if that's the case, I'll give you the money and you can walk away and we can all get back to our lives."

"It's not about money," Shane retorted impatiently, using the back of his wrist to wipe away more blood from his nose and mouth. "It's about doing what no one else has been able to do."

Trey's gaze burned. He stared Shane down. "You're not going to drop it, are you?"

"I'm not easily intimidated, Sheenan."

Trey's brow creased and then eased. "You just don't care, do you?"

"I'm not a quitter."

"What does that even mean?"

"It means I signed a contract. I'm delivering the book. I don't accept failure—"

"Even if it causes others tremendous pain?"

Shane couldn't answer. He didn't.

Trey read the silence for what it was. "What a piece of work you are," he muttered, disgusted. Blotting his mouth, he turned away, heading back down the hall for the front door. As he reached for the doorknob, he paused, and looked back at Shane. "You have one week to get the hell out of this house."

Shane walked down the hall towards Trey. "According to my lease, I have thirty days from notice. The notice came Friday."

"I don't care about paperwork. I'm not interested in legalese. I'm telling you, man-to-man, if you are here next Sunday at three o'clock in the afternoon, I will personally throw you out."

"That's assault. You'll serve time. Again."

"It'd be worth it."

"Really? Is that your idea of protecting your family? Maybe that explains why your wife almost married someone else eighteen months ago while you were still at Deer Lodge Prison."

Trey lunged at Shane. Shane answered with a right hook. Trey grabbed Shane around the neck and then froze at the sound of a high pitched scream.

"Stop it! Stop it now!" It was Jet, shouting to be heard over them. "And if you don't, I'm calling 911 and reporting an assault. Do you hear me? So stop it. That's enough. Both of you."

Trey shot Jet a hard, cold glance but released Shane.

Shane moved back but his arms were up, fists clenched, ready for another go.

"Leave, Trey," Jet choked. "Leave now. *Please.*"

And to Shane's surprise, he did.

Chapter Eight

As TREY WALKED out the front door, Jet turned around and headed down the hall, through the kitchen to exit the small mudroom lean-to.

She walked quickly, desperate to escape the house, the fight, and the horrible, horrible pictures in her head. The blows. The blood. The things said.

McKenna's mother assaulted in front of her family. Her father tortured. The children dying…

It was too violent, too awful to process and yet this was the book Shane was writing. This was what he'd spent the past nine months working on…

Heartsick, she walked and walked, passing the tractor and going around the side of the big, weathered barn. The heels on her shoes crunched clods of dirty ice. She should have brought her coat. She was cold but the frigid winter air cooled her skin, numbing her emotions.

She didn't know what was worse, either. The things that had been said or the fight. She had brothers. Three of them. And growing up they'd argue and get into it now and then, but they'd never shed blood. They'd never been so physical...so violent.

She disappeared behind the barn and as she came around the other side, a dark red horse with a white star on his forehead appeared at the edge of the corral. Ears alert, he lifted his head and nickered softly, greeting her. When she didn't respond he gave his head a little toss, tail swishing, and nickered again. She moved towards the railing, welcoming the distraction.

Jet wished she had a carrot or apple, or a sugar cube. Instead she approached empty handed, palm open. He nuzzled her hand, exhaling to blow air on her palm.

"Handsome boy," she murmured, rubbing the side of his head. He seemed to like it. "Are you lonely out here?" She crooned nonsense words while she rubbed his nose and little by little her heartbeat slowed, settling.

She could still hear the dull thuds of the blows connecting with jaws and cheekbones and hard abdomens. She could still feel the tension knotting in her shoulders and cramping her belly. But she also remembered something else, something that Shane had said. *Doesn't she deserve closure? Or is she supposed to go through her whole life wondering what the hell happened to her family? What the hell happened to her life?*

And it struck her that maybe, just maybe, this was why Shane was here, tackling this story, and others like it.

He, himself, had no closure. His past was a mystery. He didn't know what had happened to his family and this was what drove him to find answers...not just for himself, but for others like him.

And there was something else about the fight that bothered her. The fight was fierce and brutal and yet they'd looked well-matched. They appeared to know how to fight the other, as if they'd fought each other before—which she knew hadn't happened. They'd never even met until today. But they'd looked similar and they'd even moved in almost the same way...

THE SOUND OF a brittle twig snapping made her turn. Glancing behind her, she spotted Shane walking towards her. He'd cleaned the blood off his face but his nose looked thick—possibly broken—and his lower lip was swollen. Bruises were forming. He'd probably soon be sporting one, if not two, black eyes.

She inhaled sharply, battling her disappointment. "That was stupid," she said, as he joined her at the railing.

"I don't like fighting," he said quietly, stroking the horse's nose, scratching behind the ears. "But I'm not going to roll over, either."

"What did the fight accomplish?"

"He knows where I stand. I know where he stands."

"Are you moving out by next Sunday?"

"No."

She shot him a swift glance. "That's asking for trouble."

"*He's* asking for trouble. I have a legal right to be here. My lease is valid until mid-March."

She sighed. "So what happens next Sunday?"

Shane shrugged. "I don't know. I won't be here. I'll be over at Flathead Lake."

"So you're still going?"

"Of course I'm going. I've a book to write and people to interview and Trey Sheenan doesn't scare me."

She studied him intently. He looked like hell but he acted as if that fight was nothing. "What does scare you?" she asked softly.

He didn't answer for a long moment and then his broad shoulders shifted. "Losing my self-respect. I can't do that. I don't need money. I don't care about fame. I'm not interested in awards. But I can't lose my self-respect. As a kid bouncing from institution to institution, it was all I had. And it's still all I have, because the rest of it is just window dressing."

Jet's gaze skimmed his swollen lower lip, and then up over his bruised nose, and then higher to his fierce dark eyes. "You do have very nice window dressing."

His hard jaw eased. His lips twisted slightly. "Don't make me smile. It hurts."

"I don't know whether I should hit you, or hug you."

"Hug me. I've been hit enough today."

His tone was mocking and yet she saw the weariness in his eyes and felt the wistfulness underlying his words. He'd spent his life proving to himself and others that he needed no one. It wasn't working though, was it? Because no man—or woman—was an island. People needed people. People needed love.

Carefully, she went to him and wrapped her arms around his waist, aware of the blows he'd taken to his chest and torso, aware from the way he inhaled sharply that there might be a bruised or broken rib.

"I wish you'd had a family," she whispered, hands clasped loosely behind his back. "I wish you'd had a mom and dad to cherish you and spoil you and make you feel safe."

He stiffened a little but she ignored his silent protest.

"Every child deserves love, and you deserved far more than you got," she added.

"I survived," he answered gruffly. "And I'm doing alright."

She tipped her head back to look him in the eye. "Yes, you did, and yes you are, but I still can want more for you. I'm allowed to want more. You can't tell me how I'm supposed to feel. There are no rules when it comes to feelings."

"No?"

She smiled faintly at his rueful expression. "No."

An emotion passed over his face, something that darkened his eyes for a moment, casting shadows that she couldn't read, but then it was gone. "I'm not good with feelings." His voice was pitched low. He sounded as if it was a confession…something to be ashamed of.

"That's okay." She smiled up at him. "You're in luck. I have plenty of experience with them, and more emotions than most women."

"That's lucky?"

She rose up on tiptoe and gently kissed his bruised and swollen mouth. "Yes."

One of his hands slid into her hair and then smoothed it from her face. His thumb stroked her cheek, and then strummed across her lips. "This is not going to end well, you know. There is no way this will end well. Not for either of us."

She frowned, not understanding. "In terms of what?"

"Any of it. All of it. You're just going to get hurt, and I don't want you hurt."

Her chest squeezed and her breath caught in her throat. She didn't like the sound of that. She didn't want to be hurt. She wasn't ready to be hurt. But she also wasn't ready to walk away from him.

Jet forced a mocking smile. "You're not going to fall in love with me and marry me and give me a dozen babies that I can raise on our dairy farm?"

She didn't know what she expected but it wasn't the slow, long, tender kiss, a kiss that seemed to draw the air from her lungs, even as he melted her bones and thoughts and every bit of resistance.

"You're everything I want," he said against her mouth, "but everything I don't deserve." And then he carefully peeled her away from him and stepped back. "Let's get your jacket. We need to get you home. I am sure your Sheenans will have something to say to you for being here today."

Her heart fell, taking her stomach with it. She hunched her shoulders as she walked next to him back towards the house. "I'm not afraid of them," she said as they neared the back porch.

And it was true. She wasn't scared. She was upset because she was troubled. She liked Shane so much. She was more than a little bit attached. And she couldn't accept that there was no future. Why couldn't there be a future? Why couldn't they work? Because the Sheenans said so? Or because there was something else?

"Are you married?" Jet asked abruptly.

He snorted. "No."

"Engaged?"

"No."

"Dating anyone?"

"No. There's just you."

"Good." She faced him on the porch. "Because I like you. I really do. And I don't even know what that means, but it's silly to say this won't work or it's going to end badly when we're still just figuring stuff out." It was icy cold and the wind whipped past them, grabbing at her hair. Jet folded her arms over her chest, suppressing a shiver. "So don't be such a pessimist. Let's give it a chance. What do we have to lose?"

"I write nonfiction, babe, not romances," he answered, and yet he was smiling at her and his expression was amused.

He was so gorgeous when he smiled at her like that. Even with the bruises and the cuts and funny bump in the bridge of his nose.

She reached up to lightly stroke his nose. "Did you break it?"

"Probably." He must have noticed her stricken expression. "It's not the first time. It'll heal."

"Your poor face."

"Good thing I'm not a model."

She couldn't look away from his warm, dark eyes and the crooked tilt of his lips. He was such a strong, intelligent man and yet beneath the tough veneer, she could see the boy in him…the child that lurked in every adult. She had to swallow hard to keep the emotion from her voice. She was so close to tears. She didn't even know why.

"If you can wait until Friday, I'll go with you to Polson as soon as I'm done teaching. It's a three day weekend, which would give you time for research."

He didn't immediately reply. She searched his eyes, trying to read what he was thinking. "Friday dismissal is at two-forty," she added. "I could leave straight after. What do you think?"

"And Harley?" he asked gruffly.

She smashed the stab of guilt. "I'll sort that out. She's my sister."

MONDAY MORNING SHANE woke up to find Trey Sheenan back on his doorstep. Or Trey's own doorstep, if he wanted to be literal.

Trey had a yellow and purple eye, and mottling around the jaw, but stood tall, his expression revealing nothing. "Maybe we're not being fair," he said bluntly, by way of greeting. "Maybe we're assuming you understand how it works here in this part of the world. But we're a small community. Close-knit. We've known each other practically since birth. Bad things don't happen here, not like what went down on the Douglas ranch."

Shane opened the door wider. "Want to come in? I've just made a pot of coffee."

"I'll take a cup. Black."

Shane led the way to the kitchen. Trey didn't speak until Shane had filled him a mug and pushed it across the battered, pine table.

"I attended the funeral for that family." Trey's deep voice was low, measured. "Everyone attended the funeral services. The front of St. James was lined with the five coffins. Five hearses out front. Six pallbearers per casket, thirty total. All these men and boys in black suits, most wearing their fancy dress cowboy boots, because the Douglases were ranchers. Rory was front and center, leading the way, on his mom's casket." His voice cracked and he ground his jaw tight, looked away.

For a minute the kitchen was silent. There was no way

Shane would speak. He waited.

Trey continued. "McKenna wasn't my McKenna back then. She was just a little girl…skinny, with red hair. Her aunt Karen had to hold her up. Quinn wasn't there; he was still in the hospital in ICU, fighting for his life." He paused. "I knew Rory from school…sports and amateur rodeo events. He was good. I was better. But he could stay out of trouble and I couldn't."

He paused again. "The loss of that family changed everything for everyone. It left a mark on Marietta…and it made an even stronger impression on me." His head lifted and he looked Shane in the eye. "I should have been there that day. I should have had my hunting rifle, or my dad's pistol. I should have been there to help them. Protect them. Mrs. Douglas and all those little ones…they were so defenseless, especially after the attackers took out Mr. Douglas. The rest of the family had no way to defend themselves. The investigation reported that the Douglas family didn't even own a single gun."

"Attackers," Shane said quietly. "You think there was more than one?"

Trey shrugged. "I don't see how one person could have taken such complete control…it doesn't make sense."

"Unless Mr. Douglas surrendered to protect the others."

"The investigation seemed to think that."

"From the reports I've read, I'd agree," Shane said.

Trey made a rough sound. "Todd—McKenna's father—

was not a fighter. I wouldn't call him a pacifist, but he and Grace, McKenna's mom, were very strong Christians and they believed in the power of prayer. They believed God would protect them." He closed his eyes and drew a breath, and when he opened his eyes again his expression was fierce. Gritty. "It makes me so angry still. It's not easy to talk about, because it makes me feel disloyal to my wife. But you're here in this area. We're set back in the hills. It's isolated. Each rancher can be a mile or more from the nearest neighbor. You have to be smart. You have to have a plan in times of crisis, and while I respect Todd's kindness—he was known as a very patient, and generous man—he should have been prepared. He should have done more to defend his family."

"You think he should have fought back."

"I know he should have. And I'm not saying he did nothing, but it wasn't enough. Clearly, it wasn't enough. Knowing Todd, he probably tried to reason with the attacker, or attackers, first, but once he was incapacitated, the rest of the family was screwed."

"Why didn't they have dogs? I thought every ranch has a couple."

"They had two until just before the assault. Goldie, the older lab, died of old age, a couple weeks before, and the younger dog, Silver, a three-year-old German shepard, was hit by a car just a few days before the accident."

Shane frowned. That hadn't been in any of the reports he'd read. "Did one of the boys run over the dog by accident?"

"No. They found Silver lying by the side of the easement road. Silver was Quinn's dog. He was devastated."

"The easement road. Isn't that the one that cuts across your property?"

"Yes. But we never go down that way. My dad didn't have any problems with the Douglases, but he wasn't very social and he discouraged us from being overly friendly, so we grew up knowing that the easement road was for access to their ranch, not for us."

"And you all listened?"

"It was that or get some quality time with his belt. Or fist."

Shane studied Trey. "He was tough."

"He didn't suffer fools. And I don't say this to McKenna, but what happened on the Douglas ranch would never have happened here. You didn't cross my dad. If he suspected someone of lying to him, or doing something behind his back, he'd take you out, fast. And then ask questions later."

"Did that ever backfire?"

"Absolutely. But it meant he was the last man standing."

Shane's lips quirked. "You've learned that one well, haven't you?"

Trey shrugged. "I'm going to protect my wife and son until the day I die."

"And your dad. He didn't have any beef with the Douglases?"

"No. If anything he was protective of them. They were good people. Too religious for his liking but they always treated Mom well. Mom and Mrs. Douglas were once quite friendly. One summer they went every night together to the revival, and then the next summer they started going, and then after once or twice, Mom wouldn't go back. Mrs. Douglas was a little confused, but Mom was adamant. She'd had enough."

"The revival's the traveling church headed up by Pastor Newsome?"

Trey's head inclined. "Dad was not a fan. He didn't trust the minister's motives. Thought the minister was more interested in the prettier ladies in the congregation than the older ones, or the unattractive ones."

Shane's gut tightened. "Your mom being one," he said carefully, not liking the uneasy feeling he'd gotten.

"And Mrs. Douglas being another." Trey hesitated. "McKenna is almost the spitting image of her mom."

"Did everyone in Marietta attend the summer revival?"

"No. There were a lot of people who were quite unhappy that the minister set up his tent here each summer. I never went. Dad wouldn't let Mom take us. He said the minister was after one thing—pretty young women without a brain."

"Your mom was stupid?"

"No. Just lonely."

Shane didn't want to hear that. He didn't. It made him feel as if he'd chomped on shards of glass. "Why did your dad think the pastor targeted the young, pretty women?"

"Dad thought the minister was trying to get them to part with purses and their panties." A dull red flush colored Trey's high hard cheekbones. "Dad said as much to Mom, right around the time she stopped going to the services. But Mrs. Douglas continued to attend, right up until the day she was killed."

Shane forced his thoughts away from his mother, not wanting to think of her now, not wanting to think of Bill Sheenan speaking so rudely to her. Treating her with contempt and disdain. "The murders at the Douglas ranch took place while the revival was in Paradise Valley."

"Yes."

"Did people talk about that?"

"There was a lot of finger-pointing. But the minister—Newsome—he was in the middle of a prayer meeting when it happened, and Mrs. Douglas was planning on going to the evening worship service that night. She'd just put dinner on the table when the assault began."

Shane drank his coffee. Not because he was thirsty but because he needed something to do to hide his revulsion. He hated this story. He hated this book. It was beyond tragic. It was pointless...meaningless... just endless suffering and grief. He shouldn't have ever started it. If he could go back eighteen months and undo the contract and return the advance and stop the research, he would.

But he couldn't go back. He was here, in the thick of it,

and there was no standing still. Life did not stand still. He'd committed to this path, and all he could do was go forward. "Do you remember your mother, and how she reacted to the news of the Douglas murders?"

Trey set his cup down hard on the table and crossed the kitchen to the mudroom. He disappeared inside a moment, checked a shelf that looked as if it was about to fall off the wall and then turned around. "She said it could have been her."

It was hard to swallow. Shane's mouth tasted sour. "Because the ranches were so close?"

"Because Grace Douglas took the brunt of the attack. She was hurt so much worse than the others. My mother—" Trey broke off, shook his head. "I don't know what I'm saying. I shouldn't say more. This can't go in your book. None of this should go in your book."

"Why not? What is it that everyone is hiding? Because something isn't adding up. You've come here, been open with me, so I'm going to tell you that my gut says the Sheenans aren't protecting McKenna, as much as protecting themselves." He saw Trey stiffen, and a startled look in his eyes, before his expression hardened, shuttering.

Shane didn't let it stop him. If Trey was going to throw another punch, so be it. "You know your family," he added. "You know what happened, but there's more to this story. You and I both know that. I'm sure you're aware of the investigation. It was mismanaged from the beginning."

"I don't know anything about that."

"There was a big story in your *Copper Mountain Courier* the summer of 1997 about the problems in the investigation. Missing pages. Tampered evidence."

"Didn't pay any attention to it. I was just eighteen."

"But you were dating McKenna then."

"Yeah, I was eighteen, and my mom had just died. Hard to pay attention to the Courier when you're burying your mom." Trey walked past Shane to exit the kitchen. He stepped through the hall and into the dining room and stopped at the head of the table.

Shane stood behind him, seeing what Trey was seeing.

Wallpaper. Curtains. A framed landscape featuring Paradise Valley.

The bulletin boards were gone. The books were gone. The dining room table had been returned to the middle of the room, and chairs lined the table, just as they once had. The only sign that Shane still worked in there was his laptop at the foot of the table and a tidy pile of folders with a notebook on top.

There was a beat of silence. Trey looked at Shane. "You took it all down."

"I'm sorry you had to see that," Shane said.

Another beat of silence followed. Trey drew a slow breath and exhaled even more slowly. "You asked who we're protecting. It's our families. It's our memories. It's our mom. I shouldn't tell you this. I shouldn't. And if it goes into your book I will tear you apart, limb by limb, but Mrs. Douglas wasn't the first woman assaulted in this valley. My mom was hurt. I don't know all the details, only that she'd confided in Grace Douglas a little bit. She'd told Mrs. Douglas that someone had hurt her and she was afraid. That's why she stopped going to the revival. It's why she didn't want to leave the house. Brock suspected something had happened, too. He said he found Mom crying, and at first he thought Dad had beat her, but Mom swore it wasn't Dad but she wouldn't say who. Brock told us Mom wasn't well, that she was struggling with something, and so we all took turns keeping an eye on her. We made it a point never to leave her alone."

"Did you ever share any of this with the investigation?"

Trey shook his head. "No."

"Why not?"

"If you knew Dad, you wouldn't ask that."

"What does that mean?"

"He was hard on her. She was already unhappy. The last thing she needed was him blaming her for one more thing that wasn't her fault."

"Did he do that often?"

"Daily."

Silence fell and as if aware he'd said far too much, Trey started for the door. Shane followed, accompanying him down the front steps, and out onto the dirt and gravel driveway.

"What was she like?" Shane asked as Trey swung the truck door open.

Trey's brow furrowed. "Who?"

"Your mom."

For a moment Trey seemed at a loss for words and then he answered gruffly, "Sweet. Sad. So very, very sad." His voice hardened. He looked away, jaw gritted. "She deserved better than my father," he added, climbing behind the steering wheel and slamming the door closed.

Trey reversed quickly, effortlessly, and turned the truck around to head out, more familiar with the Sheenan ranch than any of his brothers as he'd been the one to work it, day in and day out, until he'd gone to jail.

Shane knew all this and more. He'd spent more time the past month researching the Sheenans then he had the Douglas story. But every Sheenan discovery just led to more questions. Like just now. The conversation with Trey this morning had been equal parts enlightening and puzzling. But then, Trey himself was enlightening and puzzling.

Even more surprising was how much Shane liked him.

Maybe not every Sheenan was an ass.

ALL WEEK JET worried about how to tell Harley she was heading out of town on Friday. When she wasn't engaged in teaching a lesson, she'd find herself stewing over the situation, knowing she couldn't just disappear for three days—Harley would be on the phone with the sheriffs and police in record time—but also aware that she couldn't just tell her older sister that she was heading out of town with Shane. Harley would have the Sheenans hunting them down in record time…

What Jet needed was a good excuse to head out of town, one that wouldn't put Harley into a panic, but nothing came to her until it crossed her mind she could attend an education workshop somewhere…something that would help her with credits should she plan on pursuing a Class I Professional Certificate. She'd come to Montana on a Class II Standard Certificate for beginning teachers, and the only way one worked up in salary was by experience and units and degrees. Harley wouldn't question Jet's desire to attend an education workshop or seminar.

After school Wednesday, Jet sat down at her computer and did a search for workshops and courses in Montana, specifically for the coming weekend, which was the President's Day weekend. She'd been worried that because it was a legal holiday on Monday there wouldn't be anything, but the opposite was true. There were quite a few offerings across the state—four in Missoula, one in Billings, two in Bozeman. She studied the offerings for Missoula, and was pleased to see several for elementary age students, including utilizing Montana state parks to teach Montana history. The all-day course would include lesson places for place-based education regarding Montana's Native American tribes. Lesson plans ranged from social studies to art, reading, and science. Definitely interesting coursework, and useful for Jet since she was still new to Montana.

Jet signed up for the five hour workshop and paid the small fee, and then sent Harley an email with details, so her sister would know where she was this weekend and what Jet would be doing.

Harley immediately replied to the email. *Where are you staying? How are you getting there? Will you be on your own?*

Jet grimaced, not wanting to fib, but at the same time not wanting to share too many details, either, which could just trip her up and trap her later. So she waited to answer, and then just before bed sent a quick text. *Going with a friend. Driving. Not sure where we're staying yet.*

That seemed to appease Harley as the next day there was no email or text reply.

Chapter Nine

FRIDAY ARRIVED AND Shane picked up Jet from her school as she'd decided she'd rather leave her car in the school parking lot than drive all the way home, delaying their departure further.

Marietta sat off Highway 89 and was on the way to the Flathead Lake so it wouldn't have been much of a delay to stop by Kara's and pick her up, but Shane knew Jet was more worried about people seeing them leave town together than the actual delay, so he agreed.

They'd been driving for close to forty-five minutes and had left Bozeman well behind when he felt Jet's gaze rest on him yet again. She seemed to be spending more time looking at him than the scenery outside the car window.

"What?" he asked, shooting her a glance.

Her eyes met his. "I don't know. You tell me what."

"You're smiling. *A lot.*"

She shrugged, still smiling. "I'm excited. This is fun. I'm looking forward to seeing Flathead Lake and visiting places I've only heard about. I know we don't have time to really spend in Butte, but is there any way to do a quick drive through the historic downtown part, just so I can see it for myself?"

"Butte?"

"I'm fascinated by the city. I teach Montana history to my one fourth grader and Butte kind of haunts me. It was once this city of tremendous wealth with the discovery of copper and the dawn of the electrical age and then by the 1950s it was on its way to being a ghost town."

"It's not a ghost town. It's Montana's fifth largest city, I believe."

"Yes, but Montana is not densely populated. Montana's biggest cities would be considered towns by California standards."

"Don't let a Montanan hear you say that!"

"No, I know. I've learned to be careful, but it's interesting to note that today Missoula's population is close to seventy thousand. Bozeman is right around forty thousand. And Butte is maybe thirty-four thousand, but it once was *the* place to live. It had over a hundred thousand people—some say one hundred and twenty thousand people in 1920—and huge mansions, theaters, and beautiful civic buildings. It even had its own amusement park, with rollercoasters and a lake and stood there until the 1970s, when it was torn down."

"Columbia Gardens."

She nodded. "I would have loved to have seen it." She sounded wistful. She was clearly fascinated by the idea of a mining company tycoon creating an amusement park for the people of Butte in 1899.

William Clark had purchased twenty-one acres at his own expense, and never charged admission. When he died in 1925, his family sold his estate and holdings, including the amusement park, to Anaconda Copper Mining Company and they ran it until 1973 when it closed for good. "I can't show you the amusement park," Shane said, "but Clark's mansion is still there, and some of the other Copper King mansions, but in my opinion, Clark's is the most impressive, and in summer is open as a museum."

"But only in summer?"

"May through the end of September. But Butte's West Side is definitely worth a quick detour. It's easy off the freeway and it sounds like you'd enjoy driving through the neighborhoods with all the Victorians."

"I would," she agreed, settling back in her seat, feet out of her shoes and propped on his dash. Her socks were dark brown with pink and orange polka dots. The polka dots and color scheme made him smile. But then, being near her, with her, made him smile. She made him happy. Maybe that was the magic, her magic. She'd found a way to thaw the ice coating his heart. He was beginning to feel, and when he was with her, those feelings were good.

Those feelings gave him hope. Until he remembered the Sheenans and then he went numb again. The past did that to him. He told himself he wanted no part of it, and yet at the same time he was stuck in it.

"So, after Butte," she said, breaking the silence, "what do we do?"

He told her there weren't many choices for accommodations this time of year and since none of the motels in Polson seemed like the best fit, he'd booked a cabin in the town of Cherry Lake through the VRBO site which meant they'd each have their own room and space, so he could write if need be, and she could work, too.

"Sounds good." She hesitated. "But how are you feeling about the trip? This is where you were raised, isn't it? At least when you were a little boy?"

He should have expected that from her. Jet was smart and always thinking and asking questions and he shouldn't be surprised she was already analyzing the weekend ahead, but he hadn't really let himself go there...not yet. His focus had been on the book, and the interview, and getting the information he needed, rather than the fact they'd be driving through the reservation on the way, and that the town of Cherry Lake, had once been part of the reservation.

Years ago Mark, his agent, encouraged him to return to the area. His agent said it'd give Shane closure, and might even be a new beginning if he was able to meet people who knew his late maternal grandmother...maybe meet someone who'd gone to school with his mother, or maybe someone who remembered sitting in his grandmother's kitchen and telling stories. But Shane had resisted returning, explaining that whatever good memories he'd once had of life on the reservation had been overshadowed by the pain of being taken from his grandmother. He'd been just a preschool boy at the time. Death was a foreign concept.

Even today the idea of returning to the reservation, home of the Confederated Salish and Kootenai Tribes of the Flathead Nation, filled him with dread, and something else...a quiet horror that made him feel too much like the boy he'd once been. Helpless. Frightened. Lonely.

Perhaps if the social workers had been able to place him with another Native American family...perhaps if they'd been able to keep him on the reservation...

Shane tensed, smashing down the regrets and memories. He was too old to mourn the past. Too old to mourn who he once was. And truthfully, he shouldn't blame the social workers; they were just doing their job. But as a boy he had blamed them. They were the ones that placed him with the first foster family, the "white" family in Missoula. They'd made him believe this would be a forever family for him, and indeed the first six months had been wonderful, no problems on either side, but when the couple got pregnant he'd been returned to the social services since they were now having a child of their own.

The social worker driving him to the next foster home had scolded him. *Maybe if you weren't so active...maybe if you hadn't been so demanding...*

Shane had fought tears the entire drive.

His second family was awful, so awful, he cried in secret for his grandmother and then the young couple that had given him up, but gradually the tears dried and he just became angry, growing to hate the young couple for giving him up, hating them for loving their new baby, their biological child, more than they'd cared for him.

It wasn't until years later that he discovered the young couple hadn't wanted to give him up, that the young wife had been put on bed rest and was simply physically incapable of caring for him. But by then it was too late to help a little boy who burned with anger, believing himself as undesirable in every way.

Of course he felt pain—and more than a little bit of shame—leasing the Sheenan house. It was a daily reminder he wasn't wanted. The ghosts of the past didn't help, either—the father that didn't want him, the mother who did, but then forgot him, and the little boy that grew up believing he wasn't worth saving.

And now he was heading back to the place he'd spent his first four years, taking the ghosts with him. His mother, his father…would his grandmother join them?

At least he wasn't traveling alone. Shane was grateful for Jet's company. He wasn't sure how she'd managed to get her sister's approval, but she must have because she was here and there had been no threatening calls or unexpected visits from the Sheenans. "So how did you leave it with Harley?" he asked. "What did you tell her about this weekend?"

When she didn't immediately answer, he shot her a glance. She was looking out the window as if admiring the Tobacco Mountains in the distance, her polka dot covered toes curling against the dash. Her silence made him uneasy. "She does know you're going out of town, doesn't she?" he persisted.

Jet hesitated a second too long. "Yes."

"You didn't tell her."

"I did." She kneaded the hem of her sweater, before confessing. "She thinks I'm in Missoula this weekend. For a teacher training seminar." She gave him an innocent look. "And I did sign up for one, so it's not a lie. It's being given at the high school by the education department."

"She didn't think it was odd that you were doing this all by yourself?"

"I told her I'm going with a friend. That we're carpooling together."

"And she didn't ask which friend?"

"I was vague."

And Harley didn't press for more info? Shane was sure that meant Harley suspected but she didn't want to know because she didn't want to have to deal with Brock and the rest of them. "You are far more devious than I imagined."

"And you're not?" She made a soft pffting sound as she rolled her eyes. "You're the one that's spent nine months living in the Sheenan homestead without ever once telling them that you're writing a book about McKenna's family, and making a million dollars off of it—"

"I'm not doing it for the money," he interrupted flatly.

"But you are making money. A lot of money." She held up her hands. "And I'm not attacking you, I'm just saying what everyone's thinking, and reminding you why they are so pissed off at you."

"And yet here you are."

She wrapped her hands in her sweater, expression unhappy. "Apparently I like you. Although to be honest, I wish I didn't. It'd be easier not to. It'd be easier to just let them kick you out of their ranch house and not worry about what happens to you."

"Ouch." He teased, dangerously close to laughing. But he didn't want to laugh, sensing it would just make her more angry with him, so he reached for her hand, and brought her fist to his mouth, and kissed her knuckles, and then again. "You don't have to worry about me," he soothed. "No matter what happens, I will be fine." He hesitated for just a split-second before adding, "And so will you."

SHANE'S MOUTH WAS warm against her fingers and yet his words left Jet cold. If he thought he was being helpful, he was wrong.

Her eyes burned and her throat ached. "I hate it when you say that," she said, trying to tug her hand free. "Why be so pessimistic, unless you already know the way this ends and you just don't want to tell me?"

"That's not what I meant."

"But I think it is. You've said something similar twice. Or you've made up your mind and decided how this plays out. Is that the case?"

He sighed with what sounded like exaggerated patience. "We know how it ends. My lease is up soon and I'll be back in New York to finish my book. While you're here until June, teaching on a contract." His dark gaze swept her. "Your contract could be renewed, or it might not. You're not sure what's happening in the future—"

"That's right. But just because we don't know what I'll be doing in June doesn't mean we know what's happening with you and me." She tugged her hand free, tucking her tingling fingers beneath her leg. "Or do we? If so, just tell me."

She heard the hardness in her voice. It matched the lump in her throat and the ice in her belly. She added even more frostily, "And, as you well know, we have things like Skype and FaceTime and airplanes and all kinds of conveniences that can help bring people together. *If* they want to be together."

He said nothing and his silence made her go from cold to hot and she blinked hard to keep tears from forming. She almost hated him just then, and she certainly hated his silence and callousness. She didn't care that he had grown up in foster care. Didn't care that he thought of himself as tough and invincible...the classic lone wolf. He'd invited her along this weekend. He'd reached out to her. He'd been the one to make her think there could be more—

"What is happening?" Shane said.

"Harley warned me. She said you were just using me...killing time...maybe even using me to get to the Sheenans—"

"And why would I do that?"

"I don't know. To get under their skin...provoke them."

"And that would accomplish...what?"

His incredulous tone made her feel ridiculous and emotional and she didn't know what was happening...didn't know why she was having a full melt down...now.

Jet stared out the window, teeth biting into her lower lip, eyes stinging.

Things had been going so well. There had been no problem. So why were they fighting now? What were they even fighting about?

Had she started this?

Or had he?

"Jet." His voice was quiet, calm.

She wished she was anywhere but in the car. "Yes?"

"Why are you so upset? What's happening? I've never seen you like this before—"

"I am upset. And I hate being upset. I was so happy a little bit ago, so happy to be going to Polson with you but when you're pessimistic and negative and say you live in New York and I live here...it kills me. Makes me wonder why I'm here. Makes me wonder *why* I'm doing any of this. Shane, I've never lied to my sister before. I'm not devious. I love my family. I love the Sheenans. They are good to me."

Her voice broke and she stared out the window blinking furiously. "If they find out I'm with you, it won't be good. You know that. You've dealt with them. You've had Cormac in your face and Trey, well, putting his fist in your face. All we need to do is throw in a little bit of Brock and we've got a party."

"I'm not afraid—"

"I know you're not. But you don't seem to appreciate that I've taken sides and that this might be scary for me!"

He made a soft, rough sound as he put on his signal and exited the freeway, turning onto the frontage road. On the shoulder of the road, Shane braked, put the car into park, and turned off the engine.

Jet watched him wide-eyed as he unbuckled his seatbelt and shifted in his seat to face her. His gaze swept over her, his dark eyes inscrutable even as energy zinged in the car, the air now crackling with a tension that made her toes curl up and her pulse beat faster.

He was so much bigger than she was. Even seated, he filled the car, his shoulders broad, his torso muscular, the weathered gray, cashmere sweater taut over his chest and arms. The dark gray sweater made his eyes look almost black and she stared into them, feeling lost. It scared her she'd come to feel so much for him already and yet she couldn't read what—if anything—he wanted from her.

Other than sex.

Men always wanted sex.

Her lungs ached with her bottled breath and her heart continued to race.

He was so beautiful and so intelligent and so intriguing...but the intriguing element worried her. Was he someone she could count on, or was she once again falling for the man who'd later shrug off responsibility, and didn't want commitments? What was she to Shane? A fling?

Her pulse pounded. Her throat squeezed closed. She was scared that everything was moving too fast, that her heart fell before her head could even catch up.

But Shane didn't say anything, he just looked at her with his dark assessing eyes, and she had no idea what he saw when he looked at her. No idea of anything, really.

Why couldn't she be a fun girl? A party girl? Why couldn't she just go along for the ride to Polson and not need to know where they stood and how he felt? Why couldn't she just enjoy a man because he was a man? Why did she need this intense attraction to become a forever love?

"This isn't going to work," Shane said finally, his voice pitched so low it sounded like a growl.

She clenched her hands, fingers tightly laced.

"We can't do this. You're coming unglued," he added.

She knit and unknit her fingers, wanting to say something, wanting to protest, but he was right. She *was* coming unglued. She had such a strong moral compass. She'd been raised in a family of strong values and she didn't want to lie to her sister—or the Sheenans. Or to Shane for that matter. And she hadn't taken his side because she liked to argue and create conflict. She took his side because she was falling for him, and she couldn't help but side with him.

She was invested. Seriously invested. And she was suddenly afraid he had no real feelings for her. That she was just a diversion.

A game.

She prayed that wasn't the case.

"We're either going to turn around and go home, or, you'll call your sister and tell her what you're doing—that you're with me and we're heading to Polson for the weekend." Shane's voice was rough, but he didn't sound angry as much as concerned. "I don't like you not being truthful with her. It doesn't sit well with me, and I can tell it's eating at you."

It was the last thing she'd expected him to say.

"She won't like it," Jet said faintly.

"She won't, but at least she'll know the truth. And if there is a problem or an emergency, she won't be blindsided. Besides, you don't want to put her in the middle, either."

She didn't.

"Are you going to call her, or are we turning around?" he persisted.

Her heart thumped and Jet licked her upper lip, her

mouth suddenly painfully dry. "If we call her, you will have every available Sheenan heading to Polson," she said carefully.

He shrugged. "Then we do."

"You don't want that." But then she saw his taut expression and frowned. "Or do you?" Something in his expression reminded her of Trey, when he'd visited the house and he and Shane had battled it out.

Shane's silence said more than words ever could.

There was more to this story, she thought, and it was beginning to weigh on her. "What is this…thing…between you and the Sheenans? It's more than the book," she said. "It's almost as if you have a grudge against them. Is it because they haven't helped you with the book? Is it because they've just blocked your efforts, turning folks in Marietta against you?"

"No."

"Did something else happen?"

"Yes. But it was a long time ago."

"And it has nothing to do with McKenna or the Douglases, or the fact that the Sheenans aren't sympathetic to your book?"

Silence stretched, heavy and significant. "No, it's not. It's personal."

Her thoughts raced. She tried to see what piece she was missing. There was something else at work, if only she could see it. "Did you know the Sheenans before you came to

Marietta?"

"*No.*"

"Did they know you?"

"No."

"Then what?" She saw his expression and suppressed a sigh.

He wasn't going to tell her. He wasn't about to confide. She could push and start another argument, or she could let it go. She let it go.

"I'll call Harley," she said quietly, "but I think now the best thing is for me to attend the course tomorrow. I'm registered, it's paid for; I just need to go. And then I can tell her I caught a ride with you. But that means you'd need to drop me off in the morning, and then pick me up after. Would that work? Or is Missoula too far from the lake?"

He seemed pleased by her decision. "It's just a little over an hour. That's easy to do."

"So we'll still go to Polson tonight? And then early in the morning you'll drive me to Missoula?"

"Or we can stay in Missoula or even in Butte tonight, and we can get up early and I'll drop you on my way."

"But you've already paid for a night in Polson."

"I can afford to pay for a couple of rooms in either place."

"I can pay for my own," she answered quickly.

He leaned towards her, his hand sliding to her nape. He drew her towards him and kissed her. "But I like doing things for you," he said, deep voice pitched even lower.

His hand felt deliciously warm on her skin, while his lips felt cool. His tongue licked at her lip, and she opened for him, nerves zinging, practically dancing with pleasure as he tasted her and then explored her mouth. Heat exploded within her and her body arched, leaning in to the kiss, leaning in to him, wanting more contact, more pressure, more sensation.

Shane's hand slid across her lap, finding her seatbelt. He undid the belt, freeing her only to pull her from her seat, onto his lap.

His thighs were hard and she could feel the ridge of his erection press against her bottom. He held her more closely, her breasts crushed to his chest, and she shuddered as his hand found the side of her breast, and then beneath. She might as well have been naked. There seemed to be nothing between them. She could feel him through his jeans. He was so hard and hitting places where she was sensitive and she squirmed, overwhelmed by the intensity and the desire.

Shane cupped her breast, stroking, and she couldn't stifle the low moan of pleasure, her nipples peaking inside her bra, the friction exquisite. She'd never felt so much with anyone. Not even with Ben. Shane was overwhelming in every way— good and bad—and her heart raced, pulse beating so fast she couldn't quite catch her breath.

With one hand in her hair, he tipped her head back to give him better access to her mouth. She whimpered again as his tongue took her mouth, and he sucked on the tip of her tongue, the rhythm imitating lovemaking. Her fingers curled into his shoulders, nails biting at the muscle and skin.

If he wanted her now, if he stripped off her clothes now, she'd find it impossible to say no.

Crazy to feel so strongly about him.

Crazy to want him when everyone in Marietta was so conflicted about him.

Crazy to feel connected when there was so little she really knew about him.

Nothing about her feelings made sense. And yet she couldn't stay away from him. Couldn't push him away or tell him to go away and shut down this thing between them.

The kiss became more insistent. His fingers had found the tip of her breast and the kiss and his touch had her almost crying for relief.

It had been forever since she'd wanted to be touched, and right now all she wanted was him. Skin. Only skin. Only pressure—

Shane broke off the kiss, his head lifting, his dark eyes half hidden by lowered lashes. But he was breathing hard, too. His slash of cheekbones glowed a dusky red.

"If I didn't respect you so much I'd rip your jeans off and make love to you right here, right now." His deep voice rumbled through her. "But I do respect you. And I've got to protect you—"

"From what?"

"From me." His mouth was still on hers. "And what you don't yet know about me."

The words were spoken quietly but she heard them, and she stiffened, and slowly lifted her head.

Part of her wanted to return to her seat, but another part couldn't bear to break the contact. She wasn't ready to leave him, not when she still needed him and wanted him and wanted to figure out why everything in her craved more connection with him instead of less.

"Are you keeping secrets?" she asked as lightly as she could manage while trying to hide her fear.

"Doesn't everyone?"

"I don't."

He looked pained. "Maybe that's why I have more than my share."

She mulled this over, and as she thought, she reached for his long hair, and let the loose curls slide through her fingers. Close, his hair wasn't black but a rich, dark chocolate with lighter sun streaked pieces here and there. "Would your secrets hurt me?"

"They could," he admitted.

"That's ominous."

His brow lowered. "I'm doing everything I can to be sure you wouldn't be hurt, though."

She wasn't going to move off of his lap without an explanation. And so she just touched him, exploring his beautiful face, lightly tracing his dark brows and the neat dark beard on his jaw. His beard was as soft as his hair. His eyebrows were strong lines over his nose and yet they balanced his broad forehead and firm mouth perfectly. He had a perfect face. It was almost a familiar face. She tried to think of her favorite actors and which one he resembled, because there was something about him that was so very familiar, and perhaps that was why she liked him so much, and maybe that was what drew her to him. The familiarity. As well as his intelligence and strength, which blazed in his eyes...

She wrapped her hands around his neck, thumbs stroking the sinewy column of his throat, and then lower to his collarbones. She could see and feel his quick intake. She stared at his mouth, fascinated by the shape and the feel when pressed to her own.

She kissed him lightly, and then with more hunger as he began to kiss her back, his lips moving beneath hers. She didn't understand how he seemed to know just how to kiss her. Kissing him made her feel so many things—and not just physical. Emotion balled in her chest, strong and fierce and so full of longing. The longing swept through her, an aching wave of hope and need, the hope and need so strong hot gritty tears burned at the back of her eyes.

I love you, she wanted to tell him. *I love you.*

But how could she? Especially as he'd just confessed he had secrets that could hurt her. How could she love someone that was still just a stranger?

But the way he kissed her made her feel safe and secure. He kissed her as though he wanted her. Maybe even needed her.

"There are things I wonder about you," she said after a moment. "Things about your past. Things that don't line up."

"Such as?"

Jet stared into Shane's dark eyes. His hands were on her hips. His touch firm, almost possessive. She liked that. Maybe too much.

"The fact that you were born in Marietta." She continued to hold his gaze, gauging his response. "Your decision to write a book about a crime in Marietta. And then the decision to lease the Sheenan house when you said there is this…issue…between you and them, which strikes me as rather suspicious."

He said nothing but she was conscious of his hands, and his warmth, and the intensity of his gaze locking with hers.

"Obviously, I can't make you confide in me," she added, trying to be patient, "but it would help since you know I've thrown my lot in with you. I've chosen to stand with you and it's not an easy place for me. I wish you'd trust me. I wish you'd talk to me. I wish…"

"You wish?"

"You'd share some of those dark, scary secrets with me."

"It's not your burden, Jet. It's mine."

"But maybe it can be our burden. Maybe you share it with me so *I* can protect *you*."

"And how would you do that?"

"I'm not exactly sure, but it does help even the odds a bit. Instead of it being five against one, it's five against two."

He kissed her, and again. "Sweet Jet," he murmured.

"Sincerity and light."

She didn't know what that meant, but she didn't want to stop the kiss, or think too hard when she was starting to feel good again.

The kiss deepened until her breathing was ragged and her body hot and electric all over.

"You are, um, crazy good at that," she said, drawing away to catch her breath.

"I like kissing you."

"And I like that you like kissing me." She exhaled, determined to clear her head. "So, where will we stay in Butte?"

"There are lots of hotels. It won't be a problem. You see something you like, and we'll stop there."

"Do you think there is anything in the historic district?"

"There might be. I'm sure the Copper King mansion isn't the only historic house that has been turned into a bed and breakfast. Why don't you check it out on your phone while I drive?"

"Is Butte far?"

"Just twenty or thirty minutes now."

"Okay."

He reached up and swept her long hair from her face, tucking it behind her ear. "And once we know where we're staying, you'll call Harley and give her an update, right?"

"Yes."

"You'll tell her we're staying in Butte, and you'll let her know you have your own room—because you will—and give her my number, too, so she can reach me if she has a problem with any of this—"

She stiffened. "I'm not going to give her your number. I'll tell her what's what, but Harley is not my mom and, honestly, the less interference from the others, the better."

His palms slid down her thighs to her knees, his grip firmed as he adjusted her on him. "You need to know this isn't one-sided, Jet. I have feelings for you. Strong feelings. And I'm just trying to do what's right and good for you. If I didn't care so much for you I wouldn't care what Harley thought, or the rest. But I don't want you getting banged up. I can take it, but I can't take heat on you."

And then he kissed her again, a hard, demanding kiss that made her feel as if she'd never truly been kissed before. Body on fire, she leaned all the way against him, hips tilting, pelvis almost grinding, trying to find some relief from the ache within her.

"What are you doing to me?" she whispered against his mouth, body trembling.

He gripped her butt, holding her to him, increasing the pressure, and pleasure. "Showing you how much I want you."

"And will you be over me, once you have me?"

"No. Because I'll never have you. That's not what this is. That's a promise." He kissed her gently, reassuringly and then tapped her butt. "But now let's get to Butte before its dark so you can see something and then we'll find a place to spend the night."

Chapter Ten

I T TOOK EACH minute of the twenty-five minute drive to Butte for her body to cool down and her emotions to shift back into some semblance of order. Jet still didn't feel wildly in control, but at least she wasn't whimpering and squirming around on Shane's lap, either.

They'd been driving in silence but it was a calm, quiet mood, almost thoughtful. She was glad they'd worked through the tension earlier, even if it had taken a make-out session to settle things. She wasn't good with conflict, and she hated fighting with him.

She glanced at him as he drove, the sweater pushed up high on his arm, revealing his forearm covered in intricate ink. The design on his forearm was just black and white, but she could see an area shaded orange close to his elbow. She couldn't make out what the designs were.

"Tell me about your tattoos," she said, reaching out to touch one of the black ink designs that looked almost like a wing from where she sat.

"What do you want to know?"

"How did you get them? Why? When? What are the designs…you know…everything."

"My curious kitten," he drawled.

"I am, so, tell me. How old were you when you got your first, or did you get them all done at once?"

"My sleeve? That's come together over ten years. I get some new ink every year, usually on or around my birthday."

"When is your birthday?"

"End of this month."

She sat up straighter. "We'll have to celebrate!"

He laughed and shook his head. "Not necessary."

"Oh, but it is. I love birthdays. Let me plan something for you…please?"

"We'll see."

"Bad answer. You're supposed to say yes, and mean it."

He gave her an amused look but didn't argue. "I got my first tattoo when I was eighteen. It was the bird here." He tapped the design she'd been looking at.

And she'd been right. It was a wing. Jet leaned towards him to get a better look. "It's a raven," she said, skimming the beak, the eye, the tight wing. She looked up at him. "Like your raven story."

He nodded.

"But I thought your raven became a swan?" she asked.

"That's here." He turned his arm, shifting to show her the inside of his wrist. A swan had been worked into other swirls and shapes, many of them reminiscent of Native American designs.

She turned his arm, following one of the shapes, coming to a long feather. "Is this an eagle feather?"

"Could be. It's also a quill."

"Because you write." She continued to trace the birds and feather and black ink that turned into a burst of orange. "What is this one, though? I can't tell. Your sleeve is in the way."

"It's a flame. The glow of fire."

"What does it mean?"

"It's to remind me to be careful. To not let my anger burn. The sun can burn. Fire burns. But it's destructive if I do."

"Why tattoos?"

"They tell a story. They are, I suppose, the story of me."

His words made her heart hurt a little bit and she ground her back teeth together to hide the fact that he made her feel so much. He was independent and tough, and yet his need to be tough made her feel protective.

He caught her expression. "You don't need to be sad. Not for me. I'm good. I promise."

"But these past few months in Marietta haven't been easy for you. The book's been a struggle, too, hasn't it?"

He didn't immediately answer. "If I had to do it over again, I wouldn't."

That surprised her and she wanted to ask more but it didn't seem like the best time, not with the exit for Butte on top of them and she still hadn't figured out where they were going to stay.

"You can trust me," she said quietly, reaching for her phone to have one more look at hotels, realizing they'd maybe just have to stay at a chain place rather than the interesting place her heart desired.

"I believe that," he answered.

"Good," she said firmly. "Because if you share something with me, I won't blab to Harley…or to anyone. I have your back."

"I know."

And from his tone, she knew he meant it, too.

Maybe they were finally getting somewhere.

IN DOWNTOWN BUTTE, Jet stood in line to order coffee from a funky, little coffee house while Shane made a series of quick phone calls. He was off the phone by the time their coffee was ready and they spent the next forty-five minutes walking up and down the historic neighborhoods with names like Granite, Idaho, Washington, and Broadway. There were huge mansions that had been preserved, and smaller Victorians that were still inhabited, and then there was a string of mansions for sale, as well as a series of older brick buildings a few blocks east that were vacant and had seen better days.

"I wish I could fill these buildings up with families and businesses," Jet said as they started back for Shane's car. She was keenly aware of the past, and how Butte had gone from nothing to grandeur—it was one of the first cities where all its citizens had electricity—to a community still struggling to preserve the past while moving forward into the future. "It's hard to see so much standing empty."

"Was it what you expected?" Shane asked, unlocking the car doors.

It was nearing dusk and night was rapidly falling. "Yes, but it makes me uncomfortable."

"Uncomfortable?"

"It was once so beautiful. And it's not anymore. Many of these big houses need owners to love them, and right now it should be rush hour with cars and traffic, at least cars returning home from work, but the streets are empty and too many houses are dark. And even though there is a new Butte, and the university, Montana Tech, this historic district isn't considered desirable anymore, and I can see why. Families want to raise their children in neighborhoods with other children."

"Should we push on then? We don't need to stay the night here. We didn't end up booking anything."

Jet turned to look up behind her at the hill with the line of tired Victorians and further to the east was the ruined mountain, once known as the richest hill on earth. "Maybe we go," she said. "Since we don't have rooms here."

"Well, we do have rooms, if we want them. They're available and I just need to confirm or let them go." He pointed to a huge brick and stone house on the corner one block over. "That's where we'd stay if you were interested."

"Another one of the Copper Kings' mansions?"

"Yes. Frasier Mansion."

"Is that one a bed and breakfast, too?"

"Like the Clark mansion, it's usually just open in summer, but I made some calls and they could accommodate us if we were interested."

"Just like that?"

"I have connections."

"Impressive."

He let this slide. "They agreed to let us have two rooms, but we'd be the only ones there, after they let us in." He hesitated. "I should warn you that many people claim it's haunted."

She stared across the street, fascinated but even less comfortable. Butte was not sitting well with her. She'd expected to love it, but instead she was really ambivalent. "Do you believe in ghosts?"

"I've encountered paranormal activity."

Her eyes widened.

His broad shoulders shifted. "Native American culture recognizes spirits. Maybe that's why I'm sensitive to it."

She eyed the hulking brick and stone mansion with the turrets and numerous narrow windows on the upper floors. "I don't know…it was more inviting earlier. Now that it's getting dark it's giving me the creeps."

"It'd help if they turn on lights."

She turned to look at him and then back at the three story mansion. "I could have sworn Paradise Valley's first teacher was a Frasier. There's a plaque commemorating a Miss M. Frasier on the wall in the small staff room, but probably no relation."

"It's not just a relation; McKenna Frasier was copper baron Patrick Frasier's middle, and only surviving, daughter."

"McKenna?" Her eyebrows arched. "Seems to be quite a popular name in Paradise Valley."

"Maybe that's because McKenna Frasier was the great-great grandmother of McKenna Douglas, Trey's wife."

"Wouldn't McKenna Frasier have been an heiress?"

He nodded. "She was one of the wealthiest young women in America. Highly educated, very beautiful, and very privileged, she left Butte for the East Coast with big dreams, but fell in love with the wrong person, had an affair—details are contradictory, but it was enough to ruin her. Her father cut her off, leaving her penniless, and she had to return to Montana, as a teacher in remote Paradise Valley."

"How old was she?"

"Close to your age, I think. Twenty-three, maybe."

"Did they ever patch things up? Between her and her father?"

He shook his head. "Her father never spoke to her again."

"Horrible." She hated Butte now. "Do you mind if we

pass on the night in the historic, but possibly haunted, house? I'm glad you've had experience with ghosts, but I'm not sure I'm ready for that, particularly if the ghost belongs to Patrick Frasier. He does not seem like a nice old man."

"I agree. Let's continue to Missoula. I'll call the manager and let her know we won't be staying after all."

THEY ENDED UP checking into a Marriott hotel at the Missoula airport. Their rooms were next to each other, but there was no connecting door. Jet phoned Harley but got her voice mail and so, after leaving her sister a message, Jet headed downstairs to meet Shane for dinner. They sat at the counter in the hotel bar and ordered off the bar menu, and Jet teased Shane about their room arrangement over flat-bread pizza and beer.

"You meant it when you said you're not going to have me," she said, tearing off some of the crispy crust and popping it in her mouth.

"I don't *have* women, and I certainly won't *have* you. And the only way things go further between us is if it's right, and we've agreed it's right, when we're one, sober, two, have protection sorted out, and three, not in the heat of the moment."

"You've certainly thought this out."

"When systems are turned on, it's hard to think clearly, but sex is serious, we both need to be sure it's the right thing for the right reasons, and I don't think we're there yet. Are we?"

She thought of Ben and the pregnancy scare and how alone she felt when he gave her the ultimatum. She couldn't imagine Shane giving her an ultimatum, in fact, he'd assured her he wasn't that kind of guy, but at the same time, there were no guarantees. She'd had her heart broken before. It could easily happen again.

"No."

"I'm not trying to play the heavy, either," he added, fingertips grazing her cheek. "Just after the whole foster care thing, and not having a place of my own, a place where I belonged, I'm cautious. Protection is huge, and the risks understood—"

"I get it." And she did. "Normally I'm the one putting brakes on things. Not sure why I can't—or don't—with you. You're pretty dang hot."

He smiled, flashing white teeth. "We're pretty dang hot," he corrected, raising his beer glass to her.

She grinned. He'd said *we*. From a man like Shane Swan that was almost as precious as a diamond ring.

Well, okay, that was going overboard but still, *we* was good. *We* had to mean something.

The next morning he dropped her off at the school where they were holding the workshop, and gave her a kiss goodbye, telling her to be a good girl and not get in trouble.

She laughed as she climbed from the car.

"I'll be back at four," he said, "or sooner if you call me."

SHANE WATCHED HER walk away from him, and he felt a stab of regret, as if he was losing her, or maybe part of him.

Until he'd met Jet, he'd lived with an icy hardness in his chest. The ice warred with the anger in his veins. He'd grown up angry and disillusioned. He'd worked hard to prove himself and the anger shifted to a low simmer, a deep seething resentment towards those who'd abandoned their children, but he'd become a success despite his fury and frustration. Success had given him a polish and a distance. He learned to detach. He learned to pretend he didn't care.

It wasn't until Jet entered his life that he realized how much he still cared. And how much he still wanted all that he'd never had.

With her, he felt good. He felt accepted. She didn't care about him because he was the wealthy, famous author. She cared for him. He felt her warmth and light in the marrow of his bones.

But seeing her walk away, even though she turned and gave a jaunty wave, made him realize how fragile his security was.

Could she love him despite his weaknesses and short-comings?

Could she accept him, and grow with him, as they faced an uncertain future?

He wanted to believe it, but it was too soon. They both knew it was too soon. And so as she headed to her workshop in a Missoula high school cafeteria, he drove away, feeling loss, and worry, and a hint of shame.

His brothers—he couldn't help calling them that now, if only to himself—he saw how they loved each other and protected the others. They'd even banded together to protect McKenna and their mother. They weren't bad people. The only reason he hated them was because they'd rejected him.

And truly, he didn't hate them. That was fear and anger talking. He just wished he'd had what they'd had. He wished he'd had a childhood in one home with one set of parents, his parents. He wished he'd had the memories they shared, even the bad ones, because those memories of a harsh father and a lonely mother had bonded them. Those memories were what made them the Sheenan brothers.

Shane merged back onto the freeway, heading for Polson. He drove with the satellite radio station on, turned to his favorite station, which was playing Led Zeppelin's "Stairway to Heaven". He cranked the volume up, always grateful for music, which could distract him from feeling, and lost himself now in the extended guitar riff.

But after a bit, he didn't hear the guitar, or the lyrics. He kept seeing himself as a boy, and he saw himself alone, again and again, with just an old, blue suitcase that he took from place to place. There were no photo albums, no special cards, no gifts that went with him. There was no one in his life today who knew him as a baby, or a young child. For years his agent had been encouraging him to write a book about his life, a memoir of sorts and, based on what the literary agent knew, he believed he could get Shane an impressive deal, but there was a reason Shane used a pen name. He wanted to keep the lives separate, and the past buried.

Or at least that was what he'd told himself.

But now after spending nine months in Paradise Valley, living in the home of his biological parents, dating the sister-in-law of his eldest brother, he realized he'd failed at keeping the lives separate. At the moment, they were hopelessly tangled.

He'd imagined that working in Marietta would give him clarity but instead he felt more like a wounded bear, stumbling and staggering, and dangerously close to roaring with pain.

He couldn't do this anymore. He couldn't maintain the deceit. He didn't like this version of himself. Living as he was, he was neither Sean S. Finley or Shane Swan. Living as he was, he couldn't claim either life.

It was time to let one of them go. He just hoped he was making the right decision.

SHANE WAS BACK to pick her up at four. Jet practically ran to the car, so happy to see the big, burgundy SUV with the obnoxious silver chrome right where he'd left her this morning.

"Hey, you," she exclaimed, climbing into the car and leaning over to give him a kiss. "So glad you came back for me."

"It's a very cozy, little cabin," he said, "but it wouldn't be half as fun without you."

She buckled her seatbelt. "Have you been there?"

"Checked in, dropped everything off, even bought some groceries."

"What about your meeting with Laura's mom? Were you able to track her down in Polson?"

"I did. There is one very nice shoe store, and I found it, and had quite an interesting conversation. She had a lot to say about the New Awakening church. She also had some interesting things to say about the Sheenans. I didn't expect that."

Jet turned in her seat to face him. "What did she say?"

He hesitated. "This is between us, yes? It goes no further."

She nodded.

"Bill Sheenan had been having a long affair with Bev Carrigan, Hawksley's wife. They lived on Circle C, and she said all the ranch hands knew there was something going on. Bill would visit when Hawksley wasn't there, but Bill and Hawksley never spoke. Ever."

"Oh. I knew that." Jet grimaced. "Two of the Carrigan daughters were fathered by Bill Sheenan. In fact, half of Marietta probably knows by now."

Shane's foot lifted from the accelerator and he looked at Jet, stunned. "Are you serious?"

"Mattie and Callan," she added. "The oldest and the

youngest. Harley told me just after I arrived. The girls only found out a year ago. It's been tough for them. Tough for everyone. Mattie and Brock were both born within a year of each other, and both are Bill's."

"This is like a soap opera."

"It is, but worse, because it's real. From what I understand, Bill and Bev had a fight and so Bev went and married Hawksley—she was pregnant at the time, and I don't think Bill knew it until later. But upset that his girl had married someone else, Bill retaliated by marrying the first beautiful woman he could find—which was Catherine Jeanette."

"Bill didn't love her," Shane said roughly.

"No. From what I gather, it was just a revenge thing. Catherine was young and pretty, and in the beginning he loved to show her off, parade her around town, especially if Bev was around."

"That's disgusting."

"I don't know when Bev and Bill began seeing each other again, but Harley said Brock knew about it, and Brock tried to force his father to stop seeing Bev, but it got really physical, they'd brawl, like you and Trey, and then later Bill would take out his anger on Catherine."

Jet glanced at Shane and his jaw was tight, his eyes narrowed. "Should I stop talking?"

"Is there more?"

"The reason Brock left home was because he couldn't stand the way his dad treated his mom. He begged his mom to leave his dad, but his mom didn't want to end up like her mom, alone with three kids, and no way to support them. She didn't want to be on welfare. Didn't want people to pity her. She wanted more for her kids and so she stayed with him."

"But Brock loved her? Was she a good mother?"

"Brock apparently adored her." She felt a welling of emotion as she remembered the things Harley had told her. "He would have done anything for her. But it wasn't enough. He couldn't save her."

They'd just turned onto Highway 93 from the freeway. Shane pulled over onto the shoulder of the one lane highway, and shifted into park. "What do you mean, save her? She had cancer. How could he save her?"

"This can't be included in your book. None of this can be part of your book, Shane."

He waved his hand, impatient. "It's off record, yes. So was it cancer, or not?"

"She didn't have cancer. That's the story they put out there, it's what Bill wanted everyone to think."

"She was forty-two when she died. How did she die then? Did Bill kill her?"

Jet shook her head. The silence stretched.

And then Shane's expression changed, awareness dawning. "She killed herself," he said quietly.

"Yes."

He sat back, swallowed hard, his hand rubbing across his

jaw. "I can't believe it."

"Troy found her. He tried to revive her. It was too late."

Shane hit his fist against the steering wheel, the thud loud in the silent car.

It was in that moment she saw what she'd been missing. It was right there in front of her all this time but she hadn't seen it. Nor had any of the others. She wasn't sure how she'd missed it because suddenly it was glaringly obvious.

Shane was a Sheenan.

Shane was—incredibly, impossibly, unquestionably—one of them.

"Shane," she whispered.

He just shook his head. There were tears in his eyes. He shook his head again, and she understood he wasn't shushing her to hurt her. He was shushing her because he was hurting.

Chapter Eleven

S HANE WAS SILENT as he drove. He had no words. He struggled to process everything Jet had said. He was grateful Jet didn't try to initiate conversation. He couldn't speak if he wanted to. He'd known his mother had died back in 1997. He'd even visited the family cemetery earlier today in Cherry Lake, paying respects to his mother's and grandmother's grave, but he'd believed the story he'd read that she'd battled a lengthy illness, and then ultimately lost.

He found it significant his mother had taken her life. It helped explain the intense family dynamics. The Sheenan brothers weren't born aggressive a-holes. They've been shaped by tragedy and had closed ranks out of necessity.

Maybe they had more in common than he'd thought.

The thought was bittersweet, but also strangely comforting.

On the outskirts of Cherry Lake, Shane broke his silence. "We're almost there," he said. "Just a few more miles." And then he told her about the town, and how it earned its name from the cherry orchards rolling from the edge of Flathead Lake to the base of Mission Mountains. He told her how the first cherry trees were introduced into the valley in the late 1800s, and it wasn't until 1930 that some enterprising farmer planted the first commercial cherry orchard.

He told her how, when he'd stopped by a grocery store in Cherry Lake earlier in the day to buy a few things for the cabin, he'd commented on how quiet downtown was to the cashier, and the cashier—an older woman who'd been born and raised in Kalispell—said the tourists stayed away from Cherry Lake in winter, but as soon as June rolled around, the tourists would return to open up their vacation cabins and cottages and run speed boats and jet skis on the lake all summer long.

Shane glanced at Jet. "I didn't have the heart to tell her that I thought the speed boats and jet skis sounded fun."

Jet smiled. "You're such a boy."

"It's fun to be a boy. Do you have fun being a girl?"

Her smile turned mischievous. "If I'm with the right boy."

"Are you?" he asked, voice deepening.

She turned to look at him and her gaze met his and held for a second before she nodded. "Yes." Her cheeks warmed. "As long as I'm with you."

The sun was beginning to drop as Shane turned off the highway onto a smaller lane that curved up the hill away from the lake. They climbed for a half mile or so, and the trees became taller, thicker, and the road more narrow.

"You're sure we're going the right way?" Jet asked, as the

lake disappeared from sight and the sinking sun was hidden by the shadow of the mountain.

"Almost there."

"It seems pretty remote."

"The cabin's on a couple acres."

"And you picked this one because….?"

"It has an interesting history, and happened to be available." He slowed to turn off onto the dirt road that dead-ended in front of a log cabin.

It wasn't a very big cabin, just one and a half stories tall, with stacked log walls and a small, rustic front porch. A stripped log bench sat beneath the front window, with neat stacks of firewood tucked under the bench seat, while a carved wooden grizzly cub stood sentry next to the front door.

Shane carried their bags from the car and set them down on the porch to fish the cabin keys from the grizzly cub's hollowed leg. After unlocking the front door, he pushed it open, flipped on the porch light, and invited her in.

The cabin was essentially one big room, a combination living room, dining room and kitchen. A big river rock fire place anchored one side of the cabin while the kitchen with the oak and pine cabinets, and what looked like a new stove, anchored the other. There were trusses in the vaulted ceiling and wooden shutters at the windows, with most of the shutters already open. The heater had been turned on, too, so the cabin was toasty warm.

"It's cozy," Jet said, giving her nod of approval. "Cute."

"There's a loft bedroom upstairs, and two bedrooms downstairs." Shane closed the front doors and set the luggage by the couch. "You take whichever bedroom you prefer."

Jet peeked into each bedroom on the main floor. One had a queen bed with an oversized red and black quilt while the other room had two twins already made up with sheets and colorful Pendleton blankets.

"I'll take the twin bed," she said. "You take the queen. You're bigger than me, you need the extra room."

"I've learned to sleep anywhere so I don't care about the size—"

Jet cut him short by marching into the twin bedroom and shouting, "Mine!" The door slammed shut behind her.

He stared at the door a moment before cracking a slow smile. Ah, Jet, his girl.

Ball of fire. Just like the glow of orange ink near his elbow. He needed to add some ink for her. Something that would honor her. A heart? No, that was too easy. It had to be more original, more profound, more Jet. But what would it be? What could be as strong and sweet as his girl?

That was when he knew he was keeping her.

That was why people promised to love forever. Because he wanted her in his life, at his side, forever.

He loved her. He knew she had feelings for him, too, but how could he ask her to choose him without telling her who he really was?

But it was hard.

He wasn't good at talking and sharing. He'd spent too many years bouncing around as a kid, one foster home to another.

Most of the foster homes were tolerable. There had only been a couple truly bad ones in the dozen he'd known. In general, people were decent and, in general, those who became foster parents did it for the right reasons.

No, he'd never been adopted. But that was as much his fault as the system's because he hadn't tried to endear himself to any of the couples or singles or families that he'd lived with. He'd never been rude, but he'd never sucked up, or showed vulnerability, or deep gratitude or any real emotion.

His social workers used to talk to him about "opening up a little," so his foster families could get to know him, and then maybe they'd want to keep him, but Shane had just stared blankly at the well-meaning social worker until the man or woman dropped the topic. Even as a little kid, adoption was out. It wasn't an option, not for him, as he had a mom, and a family, and his mom would be coming for him. So he'd waited. And waited. It had taken him a long, long time to accept it that she wasn't coming. He'd burned with anger over the lies and games. It would have been better if someone, at some point, told him she wasn't coming. It would have been better to know as a young child that she'd never return.

Maybe that was why he'd wanted to hate the Sheenans.

They were the ones she'd kept. Five other boys…

It had killed him to know he was the only one she'd given away.

But Shane was beginning to understand. He still didn't have all the pieces, but he had enough now to know she hadn't come for him because she *couldn't*.

She couldn't.

And for the first time in his thirty-four years, it was enough.

It was fine. He got it. She was just a woman…once a young girl.

How she must have suffered knowing he was somewhere else…how it must have burned within her.

"I forgive you, Mom," he whispered. *"I forgive you."* And forgiving her, he felt a rush of pure love. The kind of love he hadn't felt since he was just a small boy.

Tears burned the back of his eyes and his chest seized, the air bottling within. The years were tumbling away, the anger falling, shattering at his feet. Words he'd refused to think, feel, believe filled him, overwhelming him.

Words of love. Words of comfort. Words he was sure she needed to hear.

Blinking hard, he cleared his eyes and let his heart talk to her. *I love you, Mom. It's okay. Don't worry anymore.*

Tears weren't manly. Tears were a sign of weakness but he couldn't help himself. He'd waited his whole life to tell her this and it was impossible to hold the emotion in. Love was so powerful. It was really the only thing that mattered.

Remembering her Bible—he'd brought it from the Sheenan homestead—he took it from his satchel and lightly ran his fingertips over the still black cover. Mom.

Flipping the cover open he went to her name. Catherine Jeanette Cray.

And then he felt her. She was with him. Her energy wasn't heavy tonight, nor was it sad. She was just quiet. Waiting. Listening.

She was listening to him, waiting for him, and he understood why he'd felt her spirit so strongly at the house in Paradise Valley. She needed him to move forward so she could. She needed him to be one of her boys.

His throat ached as he touched her name penned in girlish script. *"It's okay,"* he told her. *"It's okay."*

I promise.

His heart beat hard. He wanted to help her, wanted to protect her. She'd been through so much.

You have to know I love you. I've loved you every day of my life.

One day we'll be together and we'll talk it out. One day we'll have all the time we need to make things right.

So rest easy, Momma. It's all good. I'm good.

And it was true.

He was good. Everything was good. And maybe that was why he cried. He was free. Free to love, free to move forward.

He closed the Bible, put it on the table, and rapped on

Jet's bedroom door. "Hey, babe, do you have a minute? There's something I want to tell you."

JET SAT DOWN on the cabin's small couch next to Shane. It was a small sofa, more of a loveseat than anything else, and she could see he was upset. His long black lashes were damp and his eyes weren't quite dry.

She swallowed and waited, hands folded in her lap.

He picked up the scuffed, black leather Bible and flipped it open to a page near the beginning and handed it to her. "That," he said quietly, "is me."

Jet followed his finger, saw the list of dates and the corresponding names—Brock, Troy, Trey, Cormac, space, Dillon. His finger tapped the blank spot next to 1982.

"That's you?" she repeated, looking up at him, still seeing the emotion he was trying so hard to hide.

"Or at least that's where I should be. I was the baby born in 1982."

She'd been right. She'd got it right. "You *are* a Sheenan! I knew it, I knew—" She broke off seeing Shane's expression. "I'm sorry. I'm ruining your big reveal."

His brow furrowed. "You knew?"

"I figured it out today."

"How?"

"You look so much like Brock...you fight like Trey...you're witty like Troy..." Her voice faded. "Should I not have figured it out?"

He didn't answer that, instead asking, "Do you think the others know?"

"No." Her shoulders twisted. "I don't think they've spent enough time with you. I have. And I've watched you with them. You have many of the same mannerisms—"

"Even though I wasn't raised with them?"

"Must be in your DNA." She paused, marveling a little at what he was telling her. She'd thought he seemed familiar. She'd felt strangely comfortable with him. But to discover it wasn't her imagination and that he really was a Sheenan…

"Have you known this entire time?" she asked.

He left the couch and crossed to the fireplace where he picked up one of the pinecones on the stone mantel. "Yes."

"Did you know before you leased the house?"

"Yes."

She slowly exhaled, beginning to see the bigger picture. "That's why you wanted to lease their house. Not because it was close to the Douglas ranch, but because it was the Sheenans'."

He took a second to answer. "From the book perspective, I could have lived anywhere in Paradise Valley—maybe even in town, in Marietta—but as someone who always wondered what it was like to be a Sheenan, yes, I wanted to be there, in the home I never had."

She winced inwardly. He hadn't spoken coldly or sarcastically, and yet the words were painful to hear. He'd grown up so very alone, while the rest of them had been there, together, a family. "How did you find out you were a Sheenan?"

"When I discovered there were two birth certificates. The original and the amended one."

"Sheenan was the name on the original."

He nodded.

She couldn't imagine what that discovery must have felt like. "How old were you when you found out?"

"Late twenties. I needed a new passport and had to request a birth certificate and the clerk asked if I wanted both." He saw her expression and shrugged. "The clerk was new. She didn't know as she'd never encountered an amended certificate before and so that was the first real 'break,' and it was a big one."

"Knowing you, you didn't just go okay, there's a name, that's who I am. I'm sure you did research."

"A lot of research, including a DNA test. The test is quite reliable."

"Who did you test?"

"Troy."

"How?"

"I hired a private detective to get the DNA sample. Troy does a lot of appearances and meetings out of his office in San Francisco. The PI followed him and was able to get a Starbucks coffee cup Troy had discarded."

"You tested the cup, and Troy was a match."

"A ninety-nine percent match, and since Troy and Trey

are identical twins, at least two of the five Sheenans are my full-blood brothers."

Something in his tone brought her up short. "You don't think the others are?"

He hesitated. "It's not my place. I don't feel right speculating."

"But that's what you do. That's the whole nature of your work."

"This is different."

He didn't say more. His jaw was set and he looked resolute. She knew that face. It was the Brock-Troy-Trey stubborn face. The one that said they were done negotiating, done playing nice. How fascinating that he had it, too.

She gave him a long look. "You don't want to hurt him, whichever one he is."

"I spent my life an outcast. I'd never do that to someone else."

"Maybe…he…would want to know?"

Shane was silent, considering this, and then he shook his head. "No. In this case, I don't think so. They've had enough grief and loss. They've had more than their fair share of pain. I'm not here to cause pain. That's not why I went to Marietta. It wasn't what I wanted to do."

She stared at him, somewhat dazzled and amazed. "*This* is the book you need to write. This is a story all of America—"

"No."

"It's fascinating—"

"Won't do that to them. They are entitled to their privacy. No one needs to know all the Sheenan secrets."

"What about yours?" she asked, thinking it incredible that he'd been here nine months and yet he'd never said anything to any of them. "Why haven't you told them?"

"I wanted to get to know them a little bit."

She frowned. "But when were you going to tell them? Before or after they evicted you?"

He smiled grimly. "I wasn't sure I'd even tell them. It all depended on how things went. It all depended on who they were."

She heard something in his tone that made her sit a little straighter. "You still don't like them."

"I still don't know them." He left his position by the fireplace and paced the room. "Arriving here last spring, I only knew what I'd discovered in my research. They were a wealthy, prominent Paradise Valley ranching family dating back to the 1880s. The Sheenans owned not just one huge cattle ranch, but two, with the eldest Sheenan son, Brock, having bought his own place years earlier. William Sheenan's wife, Catherine, died in the summer of 1997—it was an incurable illness, that's all the papers said—and had been buried in a private ceremony at the small cemetery in Cherry Lake, Montana, and Bill died late March 2014 and was buried at the cemetery here in Paradise Valley."

"They weren't buried together?"

He shook his head. "But discovering that piece, the burial at Cherry Lake, was important. That's when I knew I'd found the right family, the right Sheenans, and bits of story and memory came together. My grandmother had told me that my mother used to bring her other children to a family cabin at Cherry Lake. My grandmother said twice a year she'd sneak away from the others to come see me." He drew a deep breath. "And this is that cabin. This was hers, Catherine Cray's."

Astonished, she started to stand and then sat back down. "Did you know that when you rented it?"

He shook his head. "I hoped. I didn't know. It wasn't until I arrived today and saw the small wood sign hung on the back door, Cray Cabin, that I was sure."

"Does the cabin feel familiar? Do you recognize anything being here?"

"No. I hoped I would, but nothing resonates."

She knotted her hands, hearing his disappointment. He so badly wanted a memory...something to tie him to his mother and his brothers...to the past he'd lost...

"Why don't you reach out to Brock?" she asked. "Tell him who you are and what you know. Maybe he'll remember something. What is the age difference between you?"

"He was born in 1975. He's seven years older."

"So he *could* remember his mother taking you all to the cabin and then leaving them to go see you."

"Or he could just think she'd gone for groceries."

"At seven, yes, but you said this went on throughout your childhood...for four years...? By eleven he had to suspect something."

Shane stopped pacing and shoved a hand through his dark long hair, pushing it from his forehead. "I'd hoped," he said, his voice pitched low.

She felt his anguish and the critical words that had rushed to her lips disappeared.

How could she criticize when he'd struggled and suffered so much as a child? How could she second-guess his decisions when he'd pieced this much together on his own? There had never been anyone there for him, not after his grandmother's death, and she saw for the first time why he was really here, in Montana.

Not for a murder investigation.

He'd come to find his family.

He'd come to find himself.

Her eyes burned and she drew a deep breath to ease the aching in her chest. He'd probably come hoping to discover that he belonged. Carefully, and as gently as possible, she said, "Shane, they can't accept you if they don't know who *you* are."

His broad shoulders shifted, a careless dismissal, and then he walked out of the cabin, out through the front door, into the night, letting the old door bang behind him.

SHE WAS RIGHT.

Jet was absolutely right.

And yet nothing ever quite worked the way one expected.

He'd come to Crawford County with hopes—high hopes—and in the past nine months he'd learned all over again that expectations were bound to lead to disappointment.

To be honest, he hadn't even thought he had any expectations when he arrived late last March looking for a place to live.

He'd told himself he wasn't attached to this family, or even the outcome of meeting them. He wasn't a Sheenan. He wasn't part of them. All he wanted were facts. Information. He just wanted to understand why he'd been given away. That was all.

But it wasn't true.

It was a lie he'd told himself. The Douglas story was just an excuse to come to Montana. The real reason he was here was to unravel his past.

And he'd nearly done that now. Nearly, but not quite.

The door opened and closed, he didn't turn around, not wanting Jet to see how raw he was...how frustrated he remained. He'd come to terms with his mother. But he still didn't know what to do about his father or brothers.

The father was gone. Dead. But the five brothers? They were very much alive.

Chapter Twelve

S HANE MADE DINNER—A simple chicken and pasta dish—with groceries he'd picked up at the market earlier in the day. They had wine and salad, too, and it was all tasty and satisfying, but Shane was distracted during the meal, and Jet didn't press him for conversation. To be honest, she welcomed the quiet, needing to process everything she was learning about him, and the Sheenans.

Jet had come to know Brock as well as anyone not in his inner circle, but she couldn't imagine how Harley's husband would react when confronted with the news that he had a missing brother. Was it something he'd known or suspected? Or had Catherine managed to keep it a secret from everyone?

Either way, Jet hoped Brock would be positive and welcoming. It would be important because as the eldest, he also wielded the most authority, but as a loner, Brock might not be pleased to have Shane on his doorstep.

At bedtime, Jet very much wanted to spend the night with Shane. She didn't want to sleep alone, not when he was so close by, but when their goodnight kiss became sinfully hot, Shane drew back, again demonstrating tremendous control.

"This is exactly how mistakes get made," he said, his deep voice pitched low, regret in the husky tone. "I want you so much, babe. You have to know that."

"I do."

"Then we have to hold off until it's right."

She tried to smile but failed. "You are seriously disciplined."

"You'll thank me later."

"Will I?"

"That serious discipline will pay off nicely in bed."

Her eyebrows lifted. "Oooh. Sounds interesting."

"Even better, it feels so good."

HARLEY CALLED JET the next morning while they were having breakfast at a cute little restaurant in downtown Cherry Lake. "This has gone on long enough," Harley said wearily. "Everyone's upset. It can't continue—"

"What's happened now?"

"What do you think has happened? Jet, you're staying at the Sheenan family cabin in Cherry Lake, and it's seriously disturbing. First the ranch house and now the Cray cabin!"

Jet slid out of the restaurant booth and stepped outside to finish the call. "How did you find out?"

"The booking form. I get copied in on reservations after the property manager accepts payments."

"This isn't our issue, Harley. We have to let Shane and

the Sheenans sort this out, and none of you have even given him a chance."

"Oh, I think he's had plenty of chances, but booking the Cray cabin without telling anyone who he was? Staying at another Sheenan property when he's been given notice to vacate the ranch house?"

"He paid to stay."

"That's not the point, Jet, and I don't have the energy to do this with you now. I've been up all night with the baby. He's having night terrors again, and I'm so tired. Tired of having to defend you. Tired of taking heat for you. I can't do it anymore."

"Then don't. I can take care of myself."

"Right."

"I can."

"So what is the deal with you and Sean Shane Finley? Are you sleeping together?"

"That's none of your business."

"So you are."

"No. Not yet. But hopefully soon."

"Oh, Jet." Harley's sigh was heavy across the phone line. "I promised Mom and Dad I'd protect you."

"I'm almost twenty-five, Harley. You guys have to let me grow up."

"We love you."

"And I love you, and Mom, and Dad. But at my age, Harley, you were already married and a new mother. Let me do what I need to do." When Harley didn't answer, Jet added, "But I think this is less about me than it is about Shane."

More silence.

Jet drew a slow breath. "I love him, Harley."

"You only met two weeks ago!"

"Give him a chance."

"I can't." Harley's voice cracked. "The guys are at the ranch house now, packing up his stuff. They're throwing him out. Jet, it's over. He's gone. When you guys come back today, he's being chased out of town."

SHANE KNEW SOMETHING was wrong when Jet left the table, but her expression when she returned was nothing short of heartbroken. "That was Harley," she said huskily, sliding back into their booth.

He hated seeing her so upset. He hated how she was still in the middle. It wasn't fair to her. It never was. He blamed himself for starting this, but knowing her now, knowing how she made him feel, he'd do it all over again, given the chance. "I gathered."

Her hand shook as she reached for her coffee cup. "They don't want you back."

She gulped the coffee. His coffee had cooled so hers must be lukewarm at best with all the cream she'd added to it. She took another quick drink, and then another.

"That's nothing new," he said calmly, trying to soothe

her.

"But they're at the house now, packing your things." Her coffee sloshed as she set her cup down. She looked up at him and there were tears in her eyes. "They're kicking you out." The tears were falling now, one after the other. "It makes me so upset...makes me hate them." She was dashing away the tears but she couldn't catch them. "And it makes me so upset with you, too. You are so stubborn. You didn't have to let it play out this way. You could have told them, Shane. You could have done something before it came to this. It didn't have to be so ugly—" She broke off, and grabbed her purse and walked out.

He watched her go, his gut churning. He hated drama and intense emotion as it made him so uncomfortable, but Jet's emotions were different. She wasn't trying to make him feel bad. This wasn't about shaming him or punishing him. She was upset for him, and upset with him because he hadn't done enough to avoid the conflict.

He quickly dropped bills on the table to pay for their breakfast and then followed her out. She was pacing up and down in front of his car.

"I can't do this," she choked as he approached. "I want to be with you, Shane, but not like this. It's suffocating. Overwhelming. It's us against them but it doesn't have to be that way. You can fix this. I just don't think you want to."

"You're afraid you're going to lose them," he said.

She spun around and jabbed her finger in his chest. "I'm

afraid I'm going to lose you."

He grabbed her hand, held it over his heart. "Why? Because they'll demand you make a choice?"

"Because I will demand you make a choice, and Shane, you're this tough lone wolf. You don't need anyone, and I'm so scared, so scared, you won't choose me."

"But I'm choosing you, Jet. I've chosen you."

"No, you haven't. Not if you don't even try to set things right with the Sheenans."

"What are you saying?"

He felt her fingers press against his skin, her palm warm through his sweater. "I want you, and I love you, but I can't spend my life with someone who lives life on the peripheral...it's not who I am. I love kids and families. I love traditions. I love being part of things, and having fun, but I'm not the woman for a lone wolf. I'm a woman that needs to be part of a pack."

"You want the Sheenan pack?"

"I want our pack and, dammit, Shane, you are a Sheenan!"

JET WAS SILENT during the drive back to the cabin, trying not to panic, trying not to fume, trying to manage her very volatile emotions. She hadn't slept well last night and Harley's call had pushed her over the edge.

She knew Shane was watching her as he drove. She could feel him glancing at her now and then, trying to read her mood. But her mood wasn't the issue. His inability to confront his family was the issue. Why wouldn't he do that?

Why couldn't he do that?

He parked in front of the cabin and she jumped out, heading towards the front door. He followed close on her heels, and caught her on the porch.

"Not so fast," he said, taking her hand and turning her to face him.

She resisted going into his arms but he drew her against him anyway.

He ignored her stiffness, kissing her once, and then again. "You said something earlier." His lips left her mouth to go to her chin. He placed light butterfly kisses along the line of her jaw. "I do believe back there at the café you threw the big 'L' word around."

She tried to remain stiff and unresponsive but it was next to impossible when his lips trailed fire across her skin. "Would that happen to be the like word?" she asked somewhat frostily.

"Interesting," he answered, "but I don't remember like being a big word."

Her eyes closed as he found the pulse below her ear. His lips were so very talented and she found herself wondering about his discipline in bed. "I suppose it depends on how you use it."

His laugh was husky. "Is that so?"

She sighed with pleasure as his teeth tugged on her ear

lobe. "Mmmm. If you say, I like ice cream, that's very different from I *like* ice cream."

His laugh was deeper, bigger. "That is a significant difference. Thank you for pointing it out. And for the record, I liked hearing you use the big 'L' word. It felt very, very nice."

She opened her eyes and looked up into his. "I meant it, you know."

He kissed her tenderly. "I know."

INSIDE THE CABIN, Jet settled down at the dining room table to work on her lesson plans for the week. Shane disappeared into the bathroom to shower and shave. He was in the bathroom for an awfully long time, and when he finally emerged, she looked up to tease him for needing as much time to shower and dress as a girl, but the words died on her tongue.

He'd cut his hair.

He'd cut it all off.

The beard was gone, too.

Jet just stared at him, unable to think of anything to say. He noticed, too. Shyly he ran a hand over his short hair, the black ends curling up, little wisps at his nape and over his ears where long loose curls had been. "Well?"

She couldn't believe it. She immediately missed his gorgeous hair and yet what a shocking transformation. He was just as handsome as before, but handsome in a different way.

"You look like Brock," she whispered.

And he did. A young, lean Brock. Except that he had a pale but discernible scar on his chin.

Shane grimaced as he reached for hair that was no longer there. "I feel naked."

"You look good."

"Better now?"

"Not better, just different."

"I've been growing it since I was eighteen."

"You're still gorgeous. You're just a different gorgeous."

His lips curved grimly. "Okay, let's go do this."

Her eyebrows lifted. "What are we doing?"

"Meeting these brothers of mine."

"And how is that going to happen?"

"Didn't you say they usually meet up at Brock's for Sunday dinner?"

She nodded.

"Then let's pack up the cabin and make that Sunday night dinner, shall we?"

JET WAS A ball of nerves as they drove back to Paradise Valley. She tried to hide how nervous she was but she felt as if all hell was about to break loose. And maybe it was. She'd seen Trey and Shane go at it. God help them all if the rest of the Sheenans got involved.

As they passed Bozeman Shane reached out and covered her knee with his hand. "Don't worry so much."

She shot him a sardonic glance. "You're not worried?"

"I've learned to minimize expectation."

"Good for you."

"You're still angry with me."

"I'm angry with the situation, and worried, and scared. I don't want another fight. I can't watch you and Trey go at it again."

"It won't happen." His gaze met hers. "I promise."

"So how do you see this playing out?"

"I'll show them their mom's Bible—"

"Your mom's Bible."

"I'll show them the Bible and we'll take it from there."

Forty minutes later they were climbing the steep mountain road for the Copper Mountain Ranch. It had been a couple weeks since the last snow and the road was icy in a couple patches but otherwise clear. Lodgepole pine, junipers, and quaking aspen lined the narrow road.

Brock's cabin was set back in a clearing with the only tree close to the house an oversized fir. Every December Brock covered the tree with Christmas lights for Harley. But Jet couldn't think about Harley or Christmas or anything right now but the line of cars parked in front of the steeply pitched roof of the two-story log cabin.

Troy's black SUV.

Trey's red truck.

Cormac's SUV.

The only one missing was Dillon, and Jet had a feeling after this—meeting—Dillon would be on a plane soon from

Texas to Montana.

As Shane braked and drew next to the other cars, Jet's stomach did a somersault.

"Let's run away," she whispered.

He shot her an amused look as he shifted into park and turned off the engine. "Does that work?"

She shrugged, fighting tears and she didn't even know why she was about to cry but it had been an intense few days...an intense couple of weeks. Meeting Shane had turned her world inside out, and yet, even with all the stress and drama, she couldn't remember life without Shane in it. And she didn't want to picture a time when he wouldn't be in it, either.

"Come on," he said, opening his door. "Buck up. Can't fall apart now."

But before they'd even made it across the driveway to the path that led to the porch, the front door opened and the Sheenans started to file out.

Trey, Troy, Harley, carrying the baby, and Brock, Brock's twins, Cormac with Whitney and Daisy, and then Taylor and McKenna, with McKenna leading TJ.

Shane had been holding Jet's hand but he stopped short, let go of her, and returned to the car to get the Bible. But Jet wasn't watching Shane. She was watching the Sheenans, studying their faces as they discovered Shane no longer looked like a hipster writer from New York, but a tough, rugged man that looked like one of them.

Jet saw it in Brock's eyes first, but it was Troy who broke the silence as Shane and Jet joined them on the long front porch.

"Hope that's Mom's Bible," he said nodding at the book in Shane's hand. "We noticed it was gone when we were packed up your things."

"It is," Shane said quietly. "And you can have it back. I just need to show you something in it first."

Harley looked at Jet and then at Shane and the Sheenan men. "Dinner isn't for another half hour. Why don't you go into your den, Brock, so you guys can talk in private? I think it'll be easier than where the kids are playing."

Jet's heart was hammering as they entered the house. Shane wrapped an arm around her just inside the entrance. "Don't worry," he said, kissing her. "Everything will be fine."

If only she could believe him. Her head tipped and she looked up into his eyes. "Will it?"

"Yes. Regardless of the outcome, it will be fine."

"That's not really what I wanted to hear."

His mouth quirked. "I know. But I learned early that you don't always get what you want."

His mocking tone made her feel a little pang. "But you might just find you get what you need?"

He kissed her again, ignoring the Sheenans surrounding them. "I love a little Rolling Stones," he replied before letting her go.

With an easy smile, he turned away and followed Brock down the hall.

SHANE WASN'T NERVOUS as he headed down the hall to Brock's study, but he wasn't quite as calm as he appeared, either.

He'd waited years for this moment and now that it'd come, he wasn't sure he was ready for it. But then, he wasn't sure he'd ever be ready for it. Perhaps it was a good thing Jet had forced the issue.

Once they were all in the study, the door closed behind Trey. For a moment no one said anything, they just took positions, conscious of the space around them.

Shane had now met them all, except for Brock, and it was Brock who was staring at him, his hard features shuttered even as his narrowed gaze studied Shane intently.

Shane would have known Brock was a Sheenan anywhere. He was big like the others, and solid. In his early forties now, he exuded strength and a quiet, no-nonsense confidence.

"You were at the cabin at Cherry Lake." Cormac broke the silence, his tone more challenging then aggressive. "Why?"

"I wasn't sure if it was the place I remembered. I hoped it was."

"And?" It was Brock who asked the question.

Brock was definitely the big brother here, and had become the head of the Sheenan clan in the absence of their father.

"It was," Shane answered, meeting Brock's dark intense gaze. "And then I went to the cemetery and found her grave and Grandmother's, too."

The silence was deafening. No one said anything for an endless span of time. They all just looked at him.

Shane opened the Bible and flipped to the page he'd shown Jet last night. "This." He put his finger on the blank space. "This is me." And then he handed the book to Brock.

Brock didn't even look down. He just gave the Bible to Troy who was standing on his right and then the Bible was passed to the other two.

Shane just waited. This was no longer his big revelation. This was theirs. He would let them control the conversation, and the questions.

"I don't understand why you'd rent the cabin. Why the Cray cabin?" Trey asked.

"Because it's the only memory I had. Or thought I had. The only time I could see her was when she was at Cherry Lake, with you all."

Cormac frowned. "According to this, we were born less than a year apart. So where have you been?"

"At Flathead Lake with Grandmother until I was four, and then she died and I went into foster care." Shane was careful to keep his tone neutral. He wasn't here to be accusatory. They were in no way to blame and they deserved to know the facts.

It crossed Shane's mind that they either didn't believe him, or didn't want to believe him.

"We didn't even see Grandmother," Cormac said eventually.

"That's not true," Troy answered. "We'd go to the cabin at least once a year and I'm sure she came to see us."

Brock's deep voice added, "We went to see you."

Every head turned towards him.

"Mom called you a cousin. She'd say, 'your cousin Sean Cray is here to play,' and Gram would sometimes bring other Cray cousins, or Finley cousins, and we'd swim in the lake and Mom would sit in a chair near the water's edge and just drink you in."

"I don't remember that," Cormac said.

Trey's forehead furrowed. "I remember swimming in the lake with other kids. There were girls and a boy. Two or three years old, but he could swim better than the girls."

Brock nodded. "That was Shane." He looked to Shane. "You have two names because Mom and Gram wanted to protect you. They couldn't use your birth name because Dad didn't know that it was Gram who adopted you. He was told you were with a family in Sheriden, Wyoming. But Gram took you and raised you, and then she had a heart attack and there was no way Mom could bring you home. And she was never the same after that."

Cormac crossed his arms over his chest. "We haven't run

a DNA test. We haven't seen the results. This could be just another one of his stories. We don't know that he really is related to us—"

"I'm sure," Brock said flatly.

"How can you be sure?" Cormac retorted. "You were seven when he was born!"

"And eleven the last time I saw him, and I know him. I would know him anywhere—"

"But there was a DNA test," Shane interrupted. "I hired a PI. We used a paper cup Troy discarded to test. Troy came back a ninety-nine percent match. I can't speak for everyone, but Troy and Trey are both full-blood brothers."

"I don't need a DNA test," Brock said impatiently. "I know him. I know those eyes. And that scar, the one on his chin. I was there when he got it. He was playing with a sharp stick at the lake and he fell and it went through the inside of his lip and out his chin. I held him in the car while Mom raced him to the hospital—"

"Mom couldn't drive," Troy said.

"Yes, she could. She always drove when we went to Cherry Lake. Dad just didn't let her drive often here."

"Why?" Trey demanded.

"Control." Brock's expression was hard. "That way she couldn't know too much about his business. Or where he went."

"Like meet with Bev," Troy said bitterly.

Brock nodded. "It's why I left. Why I moved out. I hated

how he treated Mom. We'd come to blows over it. Mom couldn't stand him it so I left, hoping things would get better, but they didn't."

Shane had been listening to this but there was another memory whispering. He remembered pain and blood, tasting blood and someone running with him, a boy, a big boy, and the boy kept telling him it would be okay, he was getting Mom...

Shane drew a sharp breath and looked away. The boy was Brock. Brock running with him, and Mom was his mom....

"I remember," he said quietly. "I remember falling, and crying, and blood was everywhere and you ran with me. You had to run a long way, and you kept telling me it would be okay."

Brock's jaw worked. Shadows filled his dark eyes. "You tried hard to be brave." His rough, low voice deepened. "You clutched my thumb and looked up at me the entire time, and I—" He broke off, voice hoarse and then he walked out.

For a long moment no one said anything and then Cormac turned to face Shane, and he stared searchingly into Shane's face. "I've heard that story, of how Brock helped one of our cousins from the reservation. I had no idea—" He stopped, frowned. "I still can't believe—" He broke off again, clearly uncomfortable.

"It's taken me years to come to terms with all this," Shane said, trying to ease some of the awkwardness. "And

I'm still trying to make sense of it. I don't expect you to open your arms and welcome me in as some lost brother. I'm too old for that. We are all too old for that—"

"I'm not." Trey looked grim. "If DNA tests say you're a Sheenan, you're a Sheenan."

Shane made a rough sound. "And what will you do with another Sheenan now?"

Troy shrugged. "Same thing we're doing with our two half-sisters. Get to know them better. Figure out how to be a family with them. We've only known that they are Dad's daughters for the past year and a half. It's still an adjustment. Not seamless. But we're trying."

Trey nodded. "What's another adjustment?"

Shane glanced from Trey to Troy to Cormac and then nodded briefly before heading out to look for Brock.

SHANE FOUND BROCK in the barn, feeding his horses. "I'm sorry," Shane said. "Sorry to just roll up like this and drop a bombshell—"

"Don't say that again. Don't be sorry." Brock's voice was hard, strained. "I'm sorry. I knew you were out there somewhere and I tried to help Mom find you. In high school I helped her do this search—you'll find her efforts in the attic in one of those boxes with her name on it—but you'd bounced around so much and the records weren't well maintained and she couldn't find you and then they told her you'd been adopted and were happy—"

"It wasn't true."

"She said as much. She told me that she felt you, and she felt your unhappiness, and it crushed her."

Shane held the stall door for Brock as he entered with fresh feed. "Her death..." Shane didn't know what he was trying to say. He struggled with the words. "Tell me it wasn't because of me."

"She grieved for you. I can't deny that. But there were other things. Dad. His relationship with Bev. That minister fellow, from the traveling church."

"Did they have a relationship?"

"I don't know if it was ever consummated, but she carried a torch for him, for years. I think that's what drew her to the revivals every summer. I think she had this fantasy that he'd take her away and give her a better life." Brock returned the bucket to the corner. "Dad figured out something was going on, and put two and two together and created nine." He exhaled and shoved a hand through dark thick hair. "I think you were sent away because Dad thought you might have been the minister's."

"So there must have been a physical relationship between Mom and Pastor Newsome."

Brock shrugged. "I don't know. Maybe. Maybe not. There are boxes in the attic. All of Mom's personal things. Dad had us box everything up after she died. It was that, or burn them. You might be interested in those boxes, but the rest of us, we don't look at them. We don't want to look at them. She didn't have an easy life. It's hard enough living with the memories without reading about it in her diaries and letters."

The dinner bell rang from the house. Brock straightened. "One last thing," he added. "You're part of this family, Sheenan. You have always been part of this family and I'm not going to tell you what to do with the book you're writing, because that's your job. That's what you do. But I will ask that you show McKenna the book before it's published. Show her brothers, Rory and Quinn, too. That way they're prepared. Understand?"

Surprised, Shane hesitated and then nodded. "More than fair."

And then Brock surprised him again, by giving him a swift, hard hug. "Welcome home, Shane. I've missed you."

Chapter Thirteen

AFTER DINNER, SHANE went to the ranch where all of his things were packed in boxes and suitcases and sitting on the front porch. The Sheenans had said he could stay after all, but Shane had spent enough time on the ranch. He was ready to move on and after loading the back of his Range Rover with his things, he drove into Marietta and checked into the Graff.

He slept deeply that night, grateful for the quiet, and relieved to be free of the ghosts.

In the morning he called Mark, his agent. "I'm going to be disappointing you," Shane said bluntly. "This isn't going to go the way you want, but this isn't the story I can tell. I'm sorry."

Mark was silent so long Shane thought he'd maybe hung up. "This isn't you. What's happened?"

"The story is changing."

"What is the story?"

"A riches to rags love story."

"You don't write love stories."

"Maybe I should. She was young and beautiful, highly

educated, and she thought she could have it all, and so she reached for the stars and in reaching, lost it all."

"Why would anyone want to read that story?"

"She was once one of America's sweethearts."

"When?"

"1887."

"You've lost your mind. I'm sending help. Stay put—"

"McKenna Frasier was the heiress to one of the vast Copper Kings' fortunes and she ended up penniless, forced to take a teaching job in a one room schoolhouse in Paradise Valley."

"What's your point?"

"There are stories everywhere. I can write another story. It might take a year, might take two, but I'm a writer and I have a lot to say, but I've nothing to say about what happened on the Douglas ranch that August in 1996."

"Dammit, Shane."

"I was wrong to think I could write that one."

"You're killing me."

"I'm sorry."

"No, *I'm* sorry." And Mark hung up swiftly.

Shane followed the phone call with an email to Mark and Saul, his editor, letting them know in writing there would be no book on the Douglas massacre.

I have theories about who might have done it but no definitive proof, and because there is nothing definitive, the suspects are many and the motivations unclear. This is not the book my readers want, nor is this the book you want. It would disappoint and destroy whatever integrity we possess as author and publisher. I will be returning the advance and plan on covering whatever publicity and marketing expenses have been incurred.

Yours,

Sean/Shane S. Finley

After hitting send, Shane left his room and took the elevator to the lobby. Leaving the hotel, he stepped out into the cold winter air. Gray clouds were collecting over the mountains. Snow had been predicted for tomorrow.

He drew a deep breath, and then another, trying to decide if he felt regret or relief. Maybe it was a combination of the two.

Had he failed, or had he quit? And did it matter?

What mattered was that he'd decided the book couldn't be written, and it was the right decision, even if there was backlash. He was prepared for backlash. It was inevitable. He was ambitious. He'd spent the past year working hard. Trying to be more. Trying to be someone significant.

But as he faced the Gallatin Mountains with impressive Copper Mountain in the foreground, it struck him that no matter what he achieved in the scope of history, he was just a blip…he had to have perspective. A year from now he'd have an entirely different set of problems. A year from now there'd be a new story. Stories were everywhere. Life was nothing but a story. There would always be more. More mysteries, more curiosities, more tragedies, more hope, more love, more pain.

Which was good to remember when one was walking away from a huge deal.

If he lost this publisher, he'd find another.

If this career ended, he'd rebound somehow.

He wasn't afraid. He welcomed challenge. He'd known real hardship. This was not hardship.

This was just change.

And if there was one thing Shane Sean Swan Finley understood was that life was full of change. He couldn't fight it or hide from it. He had to give himself over to it and embrace it and let it take him on to the next adventure.

Like Jet.

She was his center and his future, and life with her would be a great adventure.

It was time she knew it.

THAT EVENING SHANE took Jet to a romantic dinner at the Graff. They dined by candlelight and they agreed at the beginning of dinner to not talk about the Sheenans or his book but it was impossible to avoid the topics, especially when they were still in the middle of coming to terms with everything.

So he told her how he was pulling the book, and would be returning the advance, and paying for any money the publisher had spent on publicity. He was also going to have to cover costs related to his agent, but he didn't mind, he assured her. It was better to lose money than lose self-respect.

"Will you ever write the book?" she asked quietly, her blue gaze troubled.

"I doubt it. It's not my story to tell."

"Because you didn't solve it?"

"I actually think I know who might have done it. There were some other assaults in communities that hosted the New Awakening Revival."

"You think the pastor…?"

He shook his head. "He had a follower named Jeffrey Abbot-Simms. Abbot-Simms was something of a fanatic. The church, and Sawyer Newsome, was his family. He was quite protective of both, and seemed to have taken it upon himself to protect the reputation of them, even if it meant getting his hands dirty." Shane hesitated. "The pastor had a fondness for pretty women. He had a relationship with a number of them. From what I've learned, Abbot-Simms did not approve of these relationships. He did what he could to…eliminate them."

"You think Mrs. Douglas had an affair with the pastor?"

"I think the pastor wanted an affair with Mrs. Douglas. And I think Mrs. Douglas possibly felt threatened and Abbot-Simms…" He shrugged. "It's a theory."

"You don't have theories without some evidence."

"There were other assaults in other communities. Women being raped. One woman was left for dead. She survived and was able to identify her assailant as Abbot-Simms. But before he could be arrested, he was in a car accident and died." Shane looked at Jet. "I'm putting all this together, and I'm going to type it up and hand over my conclusions to McKenna and her brothers. I hope it might give them some closure."

"Wow."

"I have no hard evidence. It could be pure speculation and wrong."

"Could be, but it's something, and I think they'd appreciate that."

"Maybe."

She smiled at him. "You, Shane Sean Swan Finley, are extraordinary."

He reached across and took her hands and lifted them to his mouth, kissing the back of one hand and then the other. His head dipped and he covered her hands with his. "You're extraordinary. You're changing me...changing my story."

"Do you mind?"

"No. It's time." He reached for the bill, quickly signed it to his room and then looked at her. "Speaking of time, I am so ready to get you alone. Or is it too late? I know you teach tomorrow."

"Are you inviting me up to your room?"

"They've given me the owner's suite. It's very impressive."

"Well then, I definitely have to come see it."

They took the elevator up to the fourth floor, to his suite. "This is quite nice," she said, taking in the living room and the dining room, and the one bedroom beyond.

He pulled her into his arms. "This is nicer," he said, tilting her face up to kiss her.

THE KISS WENT on and on until Jet's head spun and little lights danced behind her eyes and she had to lean against Shane for strength. "Dang," she whispered, clinging to him, no longer sure her legs would support her.

He didn't step away. His hands remained on her hips, holding her close. She loved the feel of him against her—warm and hard—he felt unbearably good. And then his head dipped and his lips found her ear, and then the tender hollow below. She shivered at the kiss and the tantalizing flick of his tongue.

"Oh," she sighed, whimpered, gripping his arms tighter.

"I love it when you do that," he said, voice husky. "You just make me want more."

She didn't even hesitate. "You can have more."

His head lifted. "Only if you can promise me forever."

Her eyes flew open and she pulled back.

His dark eyes locked with hers. "I can't make love to you without loving you, and I don't love and walk away." He took a breath. "Just so you know where I stand."

Her lips curled and she felt a bubble of hope rise inside of her. "Is that so?"

He nodded. "There are a lot of things we need to talk about, a lot of things to explain—"

"We've time." She rose up on tiptoe and kissed him. "Lots of time. Later tonight. Tomorrow morning. Tomorrow evening. The day after that. The day after that one…"

"I'm beginning to see where this is going."

"See where I stand?"

He cupped her face, kissed her deeply. "I do."

She kissed him back, arms wrapping around his neck, body arching into his, hips grinding provocatively against him. "Promise me this isn't all animal lust."

"Oh, there's some serious animal lust, but you're my curious kitten, and I dig you big time."

She grinned, smiling against his mouth. "I feel shameless. I love your lust."

He laughed, hands tangling in her hair, drawing her head back so he could kiss her throat. "Baby, you have no idea. We haven't even gotten started."

His mouth against her skin made her shiver with pleasure. He was driving her crazy. But then the caress stopped and he lifted his head.

"How do you feel about babies?" he asked, looking her in the eyes.

"I love babies. Why?"

"Making love could make one—"

"Good. I hope we make lots of them. Maybe not today. Maybe after, you know, we're officially a couple, but I'd love to have your babies. I come from a big family. You come from a big family. Big families are my specialty."

"So when do we get married?"

"Depends on when you propose."

He laughed, and laughed some more as he swept her into his arms and carried her into his bedroom.

An hour later, Shane proposed in the bedroom moonlight with one of the small silver rings he'd taken off his pinky finger. "This is just until I can get something made for you, babe. But marry me. Love me. Spend the rest of your life with me—"

"Yes." She didn't need more than that. How could she want more than that?

And then they were making love again, and outside the hotel room window tiny, lacy snowflakes began to fall.

Epilogue

Three Months Later

THEY'D HAD SUCH good intentions to wait, and spend a year enjoying their engagement. They were going to let Jet finish her school year and Shane sort out the details for his next book which Mark had convinced his publisher they had to buy since it was a fascinating and true story about a Copper Mountain heiress who was kicked out of society and forced to provide for herself by becoming the first teacher in Montana's Paradise Valley.

There was so much Jet and Shane needed to do but they didn't want anything but to be together, and so they decided to marry Mother's Day weekend in Cherry Lake, choosing the date not for the cherry trees, which would be in bloom, but rather to honor Shane's mother, Catherine Cray.

Harley and McKenna took Jet shopping for a wedding gown at the pretty little bridal shop, Married in Marietta. Jet didn't care about wedding colors or themes or fancy invitations. She just wanted to marry the man she loved and start a family and give his children—their children—stability, security, as well as lots of adventure and fun.

The Sheenans insisted on hosting the reception, saying it was the least they could do, and when Jet saw how happy they were to do it, she stopped protesting.

On the Thursday before the wedding, the Diekerhofs flew in to Missoula from California. Dillon and Paige and the children arrived in Kalispell. And the rest of the Sheenans drove to Cherry Lake. There was a huge rehearsal dinner party Friday night and then on Saturday, Harley helped Jet dress for the wedding.

"I love seeing you so happy," Harley said to Jet as she finished attaching Jet's veil.

"He makes me happy," Jet answered.

"He needed you."

"We needed each other," she corrected.

And then it was time to head to the orchard where they were holding the service. It was a beautiful May day. The deep blue of shimmering Flathead Lake was a perfect back-drop for a wedding. The cherry orchards were in full bloom with bees buzzing happily from white blossom to white blossom. Jet felt like one of the bees, her insides buzzed and hummed with happiness. She wanted to remember every little detail but she was too excited. It was impossible to stop smiling. And then the ceremony was over and Shane was kissing her and people were cheering.

From one of the big party tents behind them came the riff of a guitar, and the distinctive beat of a drum.

Jet turned in Shane's arm to look up at him. "Why does

that sound an awful lot like KISS?"

"Does it?" he replied innocently. "Maybe it's just a cover band?"

"KISS is not playing at our wedding."

And then right on cue, right with the band, Shane began singing, "*I was made for lovin' you baby...*"

He drew her across the lawn and into the party tent where dozens of silver antique chandeliers hung suspended over the tables and dance floor. Swags of yellow and white flowers draped across the ceiling while the tables were covered in yellow silk with white embroidery. Big glass jars held the fresh yellow and white centerpieces.

As they entered the tent, one of the band members— Gene Simmons, or a look alike—jumped off the stage and handed Shane the mic and then Shane sang the entire song from the top to her, oblivious to the guests forming a crowd around the edge of the dance floor.

It was the most ridiculous, wonderful moment of her life.

Jet had no idea if this was the real KISS, or a cover band wanting to be KISS, all she knew was that Shane, her love, her heart, was so happy right now singing to her, belting out a rock love song, and for a moment she wished he still had his long hair and the beard and he could represent the 70s properly, but then the song finished and he caught her up in his arms and kissed her, the kiss so hot and sexy that she couldn't think straight, and she was okay with his smooth square jaw and his handsome face and his lips, those lips, that could make her feel so amazing.

"I love you, Shane," she whispered, fighting tears through her laughter.

"And I love you, Mrs. Shane Sean Finley Swan Sheenan." He kissed her. "Oh, and don't forget the Cray."

"Won't ever forget the Cray."

How could they when Catherine Jeanette Cray had been so instrumental in bringing them together?

THE END

Want to read more about the Douglas Family? Enjoy this exclusive excerpt from the first book in Jane Porter's series, *The Douglas Ranch of Paradise Valley*!

AWAY IN MONTANA

Jane Porter

Copyright © 2016

November 1889

S HE THOUGHT SHE'D been prepared.

She thought she understood that it would be difficult—she'd been born in Montana, after all—but Butte was
a far, far cry from Paradise Valley.

McKenna had never experienced such isolation before.
She'd never felt such cold, either. Her fingers and toes
burned every time she stepped from her cabin to use the
privy, or head across the field to her little school.

The school was no warmer. The children told her it
would be better in May when spring came. May! It seemed
like a lifetime away.

But whenever McKenna's spirits sank, that furious puni-
tive voice she carried inside her gave her a swift set down.
*This is all your fault, McKenna Frasier. You have no one to
blame but yourself.*

And it was true. Her father had warned her. Friends—if
they could be called that—had warned her. But she hadn't
listened. She'd somehow imagined that no one would know,
and that if found out, her wealth and name would protect

her.

She couldn't have been more wrong. Her wealth and name sealed her fate. She wasn't just any young woman, she wasn't just any beautiful woman, she was McKenna Frasier, daughter of Patrick Frasier one of Butte's Copper Kings, heiress to a staggering fortune, and the darling of New York. And because she was highly prized on the marriage mart, because she was beautiful and wealthy and virginal, she could only be seen in the right places, with the right people, and under no circumstances could she ever be touched. Or almost touched. Or suspected of being touched. Because once touched, beautiful virginal heiresses were forever ruined.

And in McKenna's case, disinherited.

For updates from Jane, check out janeporter.com

Love alpha heroes? Check out *New York Times* bestselling
author Jane Porter's series...

THE TAMING OF THE SHEENANS

Christmas at Copper Mountain
Book 1: Brock Sheenan's story

The Tycoon's Kiss
Book 2: Troy Sheenan's story

The Kidnapped Christmas Bride
Book 3: Trey Sheenan's story

The Taming of the Bachelor
Book 4: Dillion Sheenan's story

A Christmas Miracle for Daisy
Book 5: Cormac Sheenan's story

The Lost Sheenan's Bride
Book 6: Shane Sheenan's story

Available at your favorite online retailer!

ABOUT THE AUTHOR

New York Times and USA Today bestselling author of more than fifty romances and women's fiction titles, **Jane Porter** has been a finalist for the prestigious RITA award five times and won in 2014 for Best Novella with her story, Take Me, Cowboy, from Tule Publishing. Today, Jane has over 12 million copies in print, including her wildly successful, Flirting With Forty, picked by Redbook as its Red Hot Summer Read, and reprinted six times in seven weeks before being made into a Lifetime movie starring Heather Locklear. A mother of three sons, Jane holds an MA in Writing from the University of San Francisco and makes her home in sunny San Clemente, CA with her surfer husband and two dogs.

Visit Jane at JanePorter.com.

Thank you for reading

THE LOST SHEENAN'S BRIDE

If you enjoyed this book, you can find more from all our great authors at TulePublishing.com, or from your favorite online retailer.